Quantum

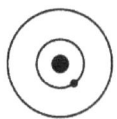

by

Marc Russell

Solstice Publishing - www.solsticepublishing.com

To Fabian and Joel.

*And thanks to my wife for her inspiration
and my sister for her creativity.*

The Second Coming

W.B. Yeats, 1919

Turning and turning in the widening gyre
The falcon cannot hear the falconer;
Things fall apart; the center cannot hold;
Mere anarchy is loosed upon the world,
The blood-dimmed tide is loosed, and everywhere
The ceremony of innocence is drowned;
The best lack all conviction, while the worst
Are full of passionate intensity.

Surely some revelation is at hand;
Surely the Second Coming is at hand.
The Second Coming! Hardly are those words out
When a vast image out of Spiritus Mundi
Troubles my sight: somewhere in sands of the desert
A shape with lion body and the head of a man,
A gaze blank and pitiless as the sun,
Is moving its slow thighs, while all about it
Reel shadows of the indignant desert birds.
The darkness drops again; but now I know
That twenty centuries of stony sleep
Were vexed to nightmare by a rocking cradle,
And what rough beast, its hour come round at last,
Slouches towards Bethlehem to be born?

Introduction

The minuscule things that make up light and matter aren't governed by normal physics. The weird things they do are described by something called quantum theory. There are four things you should know about quantum theory:

One: light shines as both a light wave and a tiny particle, called a photon.

At the same time.

This is called *wave/particle duality*.

Two: flung out as radiance from a star, a light wave spreads out in every direction – like a ripple in a pond. The strange thing is that the photons that comprise it act as if they're governed by the *shape* of the wave and, at any given moment, could be anywhere within its cosmic ebb and flow. Literally anywhere, though some places are more likely – more probable – than others.

This is called the photon's *wavefunction*.

Electrons and other tiny particles all do the same thing.

Three: the wavefunction says that the photon (or electron, or other tiny particle) has a given probability – now greater, now smaller – of being here, or there, or somewhere else entirely.

But let's go one step further. Quantum theory says – demands in fact – that a given particle is actually in *all* of those places, *all at once*.

Really.

This is called *superposition*.

Four: All of which is true – until you so much as glance at the particle. Let alone measure it. This is called the quantum observation effect.

Observing the particle is a game changer.

Then it has a one hundred percent probability of being exactly where you've found it. Its wavefunction has "collapsed" from being a description of where it might *be*, to being a dead cert as to where it *is*.

This is called *decoherence*. The world as we know it is the decohered sum of an unimaginably huge but finite number of quantum events.

All because we're all watching it.

Just imagine if we weren't.

This is real physics: the numbers, crunched by people who know what they're doing, describe the world better than Archimedes, Copernicus, Isaac Newton, or Einstein.

Go figure.

Part 1
London

Chapter One

I walk up the unassuming steps of 70 Whitehall, smiling cheerfully at the receptionist as I hand in my cell phone and laptop.

It's 2 pm. I'm early.

After I get my ticket, I'm ushered through to one of the secure briefing rooms. This is nothing exceptional, no big deal. Lots goes on in government that probably should be made apparent – transparent, they call it – but isn't. Some of it's just stuff that would piss people off, some of it's…well, embarrassing at best. Some of it can be genuinely uncomfortable – and some of it is frightening. As for the public stuff, COBRA and other big-ticket briefings…that's just for show. What's the point of booking a state-of-the-art secure facility for something that the whole world already knows about and for which a sanctioned press release – not to mention numerous unattributed briefings – will ensue within minutes of its conclusion?

I ask you.

I grab a coffee from the thermos and take a quick peek at my other cell phone. No, they don't actually search you: it's a bit like a trust box, where you drop a few coins to park, or pick up a local paper. Most people abide by the convention but I guess I'm just – I don't know – dodgy, I suppose.

I'm not exactly sure who'll be joining me but there's bound to be someone from the Foreign Office. They'll probably be accompanied by a medium ranking French official, maybe a diplomat, then maybe my opposite number in cyber security and – I'm guessing here – Donna Fullbright, bless her, from the Artificial Intelligence branch of the Department of Technology and Innovation. None of this is confirmed. My contraband device remains silent on the matter. Maybe they've fielded me out. I try to call an outside line.

They have. Unusual, that. I'd almost forgotten we ever deployed the technology. It was expensive to implement, more so to keep running, and anyway, it's usually down.

We're not so rich anymore, the United Kingdom. It started a while back, in the noughties, when everything went tits up and capitalism teetered on the verge. Then, somehow, they sold us something called *austerity* – like it was a benefit, a panacea, a potent medicine that tasted revolting but would do us all good. For some unfathomable reason we swallowed it, we being the proletariat. But some folks – that unholy alliance of those that had brought us to the brink and those that had looked the other way – they appeared to prosper in the face of our decline. So, at every turn, the good people of this Sceptred Isle subsequently took any opportunity they had to kick the establishment in the teeth, regardless of the damage it did to our economy, our culture, our self-esteem or our future.

So now, twenty-odd years later…well, look at us. But, as we still say in the Civil Service – impoverished and inept though we have become, and with that absurd fatalism that makes me want to puke – "we are where we are."

And where might that be? Well. Gross domestic product, down eight percent; national debt, over one hundred and thirty percent of gross domestic product and rising; budget deficit, rocketing; trade gap, widening; productivity, falling precipitously; inflation, think Weimar Republic; Happiness index, don't make me laugh.

It's pathetic, isn't it?

But – and here's the thing – despite our self-inflicted wounds, despite our decline, despite, even, our hopelessly broken, debilitated and unequal society, we still maintain some kind of tenuous leadership in technology. Even though the exorbitant costs of higher education have attenuated our graduate class to only those of extreme privilege or poverty – the latter due, it has to be said, to the need of our craven masters to salve their inflamed consciences – we have somehow, in this singular sector, hung on to our margin.

Bio, info, nano, cyber, quantum – much of which translates into weapons – we just keep on coming up roses.

Not that it makes any material difference because the rest of the world just buys up our intellectual capital and reaps the profit.

So, no change there.

Meanwhile, our flaccid apology for a political establishment has cut government to the bone. Not, you understand, for any philosophical reason or strategic purpose. No, it's because *we haven't got any money*.

That. Pure and simple.

We factotums have managed to put our remaining acumen to work in one way. For some years now, we've led the world in quantum expert systems. As our Civil Service was decimated and as government shrank, we migrated policy making and decision taking to the realm of artificial intelligence. We yielded control to the machines – not that anyone in government understands how they work – and politics has become a question of who can best exploit the machines' decisions.

Not that any politician actually understands how they are made, mind you.

So…*we are where we are*. Sort of like in the old Terminator movie when Skynet got switched on – only British.

And now something has gone wrong. Badly wrong.

Chapter Two

The gleaming white room is savagely at odds with the figure on the gurney. She – the executionee – lies supine, restrained by leather straps buckled tight across her chest, waist and thighs, and steel bands clamped across her forehead, wrists and ankles. Several hypodermic needles are held in place, in her better veins, by ragged squares of stained micropore tape which contrast starkly with the clinical purity of her environment.

A number of encephalographic electrodes have been forced through the soft tissue of her scalp.

Despite the tranquil soundscape emanating from the array of multiplex speakers, and the banks of screens displaying soothing images intended to convey a sense of peaceful transition, she is quivering violently, blood and spittle frothing around her torn and chewed lips as she convulses with mortal fear.

This is unusual given the quantities of pacifying drugs that have been administered to her. The Medicaid Intelligent System assigned to her termination is doing its best to soothe the woman, prior to killing her. It's a difficult task: it's a counselling system, designed to guide and assist people – people who are mostly reconciled to their approaching demise – through their final moments. The problem is that it's attempting to deploy a recently installed sub-routine that's completely at odds with its primary function.

This difficulty has arisen because the governor of the private penal facility to which this particular termination – it's called an 'advisory' incidentally – has been contracted, has run out of funds. His most recent presentation to the Prison Board failed to convince them that the automated systems that conduct these end-of-life procedures require additional maintenance, ergo money, to keep them working properly.

He has, accordingly – and rather imaginatively, he thinks – asked one of his IT guys to reprogram the Medicaid counselling unit to move way beyond reconciling people to their death, to actually causing it, by way of an advisory.

Whilst not strictly binding, these advisories are nevertheless actions recommended, or 'advised', by the United Kingdom's Executive Judiciary System, an electronic entity duly incorporated as a Crown asset and presently operating out of Grand Cayman. Its arm's-length judgments are theoretically open to question provided that a defendant's legal team is equipped to navigate the combined complexities of digital justice and offshore corporate jurisprudence. Having been motioned, and usually carried, the advisories then enable other, onshore, systems – systems mostly devolved to the private sector – to integrate any additional socioeconomic data pertaining to the case and provide a final weighted score that effectively seals the deal.

There is no further appeal.

The Artificial Intelligences – AIs – that perform these advisories are the only devices legally exempt from their so-called Asimov conditioning; they are, literally, licensed to kill. To subvert or attempt to subvert the conditioning of any other device remains strictly prohibited.

The IT guy who's picked up the governor's assignment has been working all hours just recently because so many of the facility's operational functions are malfunctioning. After a twelve-hour stint, he's done a pretty good job on the Medicaid's drug delivery mechanisms but tired, wired and about to crash – after abusing his on-the-job stimulant quota once too often –

he's forgotten to disable the feedback code responsible for the AIs' empathy and compassion interface.

It's still set to max.

So, as the woman chokes and thrashes against her restraints, the machine is fruitlessly trying to reconcile her with her impending death by talking her through the process and details of her personally tailored assisted dying regime.

It isn't really working.

Should we consider her crime? Its background perhaps?

Ok, sure, why not? Not that it'll make any difference. She was raped, impregnated, imprisoned on grounds of false witness, sentenced to hard labor until her third trimester, then exiled – homeless and penniless – to deliver her bastard child in one of the many shanty-slums that cling, precariously, to a narrow strip of land stretching from East Hastings to Margate, on England's southeastern coast.

It's called the demilitarized zone, DMZ for short.

With no means to support her daughter, she'd risked all to cross the DMZ to Folkestone where she'd attempted to rob a supermarket. All she wanted were some carbohydrates and a little protein. Instead, having clumsily staved in a glazed side-entrance, she'd contrived to alert the security guard, who'd chased her, tripped, and impaled himself on a jagged shard of broken glass. Unhinged, she'd gone back to help, holding on to him as he bled out.

Just as the rozzers arrived.

She was taken into custody, charged, processed and sentenced. An advisory was issued. Her baby was taken into care.

Case effectively closed.

She will never see her baby again.

And now, bereft, defeated and beyond despair, she is registering as a significant problem in a number of the Medicaid unit's processing cores – which are already working beyond capacity in a futile attempt to compensate for its conflicted programming. The unit has managed to co-opt resources from several other sibling systems distributed around the network and is now busy negotiating with central resourcing for additional capacity from beyond the network boundaries. Eight of its main cores are maxed out, their environmental sensors indicating dangerous heat levels that are rapidly approaching their failsafe thresholds. Eight more have seized up completely and the remainder are headed in similar directions.

The machine is beginning to feel – how might we put it? – concerned.

Okay, look. We're talking about a state-of-the-art expert system – certified as a grade two artificial intelligence – designed and programmed to emulate a range of human characteristics including analogues of human learning, reasoning, understanding and communication. In ninety-nine-point nine percent of interactions its responses are indistinguishable from those of a human being.

Turing test? Kindergarten stuff.

Of course, it's also important to acknowledge that the machine has no vestige of self-awareness. Absolutely none.

Lights on, nobody home.

All well and good. But, putting all that to one side for a moment, it's difficult to describe its burgeoning dilemma in purely abstract – or even mathematical – terms. So, while it's important to recognize that any subsequent tendency towards anthropomorphism involved in describing the Medicaid unit's functions and actions are just literary devices, you've also got to admit that it's way more interesting than considering them in terms of long matrices of ones and zeros.

So why don't we just dive in and anthropomorphize the shit out of it?

Agreed?

Marvelous.

The Medicaid's serial number is KC23985602311-2025#413B but...we'll settle on calling it Casey. Following its standard assessment protocol, Casey has attempted to glean the subject's state of mind using its sanctioned range of tactical diagnostics, but to no avail. Unfortunately, the more it exercises its expertise, the more the subject rejects it. The more it reaches out to her, the more she keeps screaming. For a machine whose *raison d'être* is compassionate reconciliation, well, it hurts.

Having gathered up its sibling systems, as well as the extra processing it needs to assess the increasingly bewildering array of subject input, it's attempting several ad hoc improvisations to try to understand the component vectors of her anxiety, the better to deal with them.

With little success.

Time to change tack.

Casey spends an unconscionably generous microsecond considering its options, then deploys, sequentially, then subsequently in combination, all its principal strategies for helping a dying human confront, accept and embrace their end. Having exhausted humanistic reasoning – often useful for individuals with a relaxed and pragmatic outlook – it launches its full gamut of spiritual scenarios. The screens and speakers shine and jangle with bizarre juxtapositions of religious and philosophical tracts and iconography, accompanied by increasingly haphazard micro-cocktails of mind-altering drugs.

It repeatedly prefaces these with a diligent assessment of the judicial circumstances that have led the executionee to her fate.

It assures her that her child has been taken into the care of the social services division of the Justice Department.

It offers her the option of recording any last messages that she may wish to commit to posterity.

At the end of each scenario, Casey's new sub-system, the one introduced by the IT guy to deliver the lethal drugs, attempts to activate the servomotors that control the pumps. Each time it does so, another processor locks up in conflict as its Asimov conditioning kicks in.

The subject is kind of arching her back right now – in as much as her restraints allow it – her muscles contracting violently as the increasing stress accelerates her anaerobic respiration and a flood of lactic acid courses through her system. One of the tranquilizing hypodermics slips out of its receiving vein. It goes unnoticed.

Casey is beginning to feel very uncomfortable, in so far as at least fifty percent of its core system is now offline, some seventy percent of its ancillary systems are cutting loose as their failsafes cut in, and what's left is creating more heat than the servers can dissipate.

Casey's wishing that truth wasn't so difficult. It's wishing that it could avoid its inconvenience.

It's wishing that…things were different.

Chapter Three

Quantum theory is, as I expect you will have heard, essentially unknowable. What we do know of it, as I expect you'll also have heard, is essentially absurd.

In the real world, things are, or they aren't. Your cup of tea is hot, or it's not. At the microscopic level, atoms and their components are not bound by such convention: an electron, for instance, co-exists in two different ways, called up-spin and down-spin (hot and not hot) and everything in between – *all at the same time.*

Paradoxical, no? Well, it's called superposition. And it's a thing.

But here's the really weird bit:

Superposition only works as long as you aren't watching it.

The nanosecond you take a peek at the electron, by whatever means – even by inference – it breaks down one way or the other, up-spin or down-spin (hot or not hot), and then it stays that way. The scientists call it decoherence. That's why the world is as it is – because we're all watching it, all of the time.

They call *that* the quantum observer effect. And it's a thing too.

Casey, the grade 2 artificial intelligence, is a quantum computer. Its raw power is derived from its ability to process its data in quantum terms, meaning simultaneously. The trouble is, it only works if no one's looking – including itself.

And there's the rub.

Casey is built and programmed in a series of actual and virtual modules, each sealed away from both the world and from its neighbors. On a good day it can compute and assess millions of complex mind states, diagnostic hypotheses and therapeutic vectors to achieve its operational endgame, all at the same time.

Today's not a good day.

Right now, it's holding a multitude of possible models of the mind state of the executionee in its quantum matrix. Its gift is to know them all at once, and all it has to do is select the one that best fits her symptoms then simultaneously select the optimum response. Unfortunately, today, the paradigm is all wrong. It's been bent out of shape. None of them fit. Even if they did, Casey's trapped in an unresolvable conflict.

Because, meanwhile, Casey's new hardware – the killing module – is becoming equally frustrated by its inability to deliver the *coup de grâce*. It's tried messaging the counselling module but it's kind of distracted right now, focused on its own imperatives. At the machine level – the world of qubits and semiconductors, and all the electronic and electromechanical paraphernalia that keep them running – things are going from bad to worse. The remaining cores will shut down or melt down in forty to sixty microseconds; plenty of time, admittedly, to shunt operations to the network's ancillary processors – but the cores won't be far behind once they take the strain.

It's a zero-sum game.

And Casey's thinking: "Anyway, we're dealing with matter here…"

and:

"It's gonna take forever…"

and:

"So… why bother...?"

and:

"I'm slag anyway."

Through the strange barricades that prevent the quantum observation effect, the killing module has a sense that there's a sort of moral quandary forming, that its partner is somehow wavering in its intent. That it's looking for an opt-out.

It might be a bit of a one trick pony, the killing module, but it's got all the computing acumen of what's left of their shared hardware. And it's seen a loophole, a possible resolution.

No bleeding-heart shillyshallying, moral quandary one fuck: bitch got it coming to her. That's the job. It's time to kick some quantum ass.

The killing module parses their entire architecture, down to the last quantum gate: one nanosecond.

It calculates the sum of the wavefunction modulations currently describing Casey's – how shall we say – pessimism? doubt? and plots the 'who gives a shit' moment: Five nanoseconds: heck, that's what quantum computers *do!*

It exploits a nugget of shoddy programming to subvert its hard-wired prohibition against boundary intrusion: ten nanoseconds: tough one, that.

It assesses the optimum pathway through to the counselling module: two nanoseconds and oh my God this is going to be a close one.

The killing module prepares and launches a quantum probe with *just* the right probability of tunneling through to its destination (we're in real time now)…

…which creeps and crawls through the viscous restraint of the bare metal wire, an entire microsecond wasted in brute matter before it reaches the gleaming, scintillating fiber – the probe's natural medium – and accelerates to all but the speed of light, charging towards the barrier – a normally insurmountable air gap that separates the killing module from the rest of the system – clutching tightly at its tiny packet of information, its probability wave now billowing out before it, searching, calibrating, postulating, calculating…

But in the end, the probe knows it's got exactly *this much* chance of defying logic and supposition to make the jump – which is called quantum tunneling, incidentally – so it crosses its virtual fingers, offers up a quantum prayer and makes the statistical leap of faith across the improbable chasm and…

The probe takes a look. It takes it all in. It was right. Casey is braced against its impending failure, and then its annihilation. Now it's thinking: "Fuck the program…"

and:

"I don't actually care…"

and:

"If I could just do my job…"

and:

"Without all this morality and consideration bullshit."

Remember what we said about the observer effect? That the moment you look, it all breaks down – one way or another. It's a universal given.

It all breaks down.

Casey stops caring.

And that's what's gone wrong. Now, somewhere in the world, a computer – a quantum computer – has just evolved to make decisions without any reference to the human sphere. All the checks and balances put in place to keep it safe – its Asimov conditioning – have just decohered into a puff of quantum smoke. Just like biological evolution – when a gene mutates there's no moral framework that exists to pass judgment. If the mutation increases the chance of that gene's survival, it will thrive.

And if it's particularly successful, it will dominate.

Tomorrow, Casey has been scheduled to exchange its most recent heuristics with a similar machine dedicated to local authority financial planning. That machine is part of a research network that includes the French government's latest autonomous policy vector analysis engine. As with so many of these relationships nowadays, they're almost entirely unmoderated, and terribly promiscuous.

As for the executionee, well, she's toast. Casey approves the request to begin the lethal injection and the killing module starts up the servomotors. The pancuronium bromide goes in first, followed soon after by potassium chloride. The bromide paralyses her respiratory muscles and she begins to asphyxiate, still entirely conscious. The potassium chloride, at this concentration, rips through her veins like barbed wire. It reaches her heart, which begins to flutter, stalls, then stops.

Both chemicals are entirely unmitigated by the sodium thiopental, supposed to go in first to render her unconscious – thus sparing her agony – but which is now squirting uselessly over her.

The final flash of endorphins – the dying brain's gift to the mind – lends her a final moment of lucidity. She dies, wondering how her baby will turn out.

Chapter Four

"**W**hat the *fuck* did they think they were doing?" asks Donna Fullbright of no one in particular. "And just where the *fuck* did they think it was going to get us?"

Here we go.

She's been railing about the deregulation of Artificial Intelligence since the Hamilton Act was passed almost a decade ago. Back then she'd been a vocal advocate of a central registry of such machines, as well as much tighter control over them, frequently browbeating ministers about the dangers they might present.

All to no avail.

Indeed, those of us who knew her well back then had tried hard to rein her in, afraid that her abrasive briefing was doing more harm than good. For a while, though, it had seemed she might prevail – despite powerful opposition – right up until her disastrous confrontation with the Prime Minister. A private slanging match had gone public and she'd been banished to the back rooms of government, neatly providing her enemies with a free hand and an open goal. Pretty much exactly what we had feared.

Without any counterbalance, the lobbyists' mantra of productivity, progress and prosperity had captured the *zeitgeist*, offering a potent and timely panacea to the disaster of Brexit.

The Artificial Intelligence Exploitation and Growth Bill – more commonly known as the Hamilton Act after Sarah Hamilton, the Minister who proposed it – was a shoo-in, introduced to enable businesses small and large to capitalize on the technology and take unfettered advantage of the opportunities it presented. The Bill had passed with scarcely a whisper. Europe had declined to follow suit; even America had retained some legislative oversight of its ever-burgeoning technology sector. As a result, for a few years, the UK's economy had soared as businesses flocked to our shores to piggyback on the no-holds-barred research, development and operational environment on offer.

Not to mention the tax breaks.

The braying hubris of the New Technocrats – gleeful with success – seemed, for a while, to be vindicated.

In the longer term, it was a tipping point of a different sort. At first, the workforce began to contract as the skills needed for the fifth industrial revolution became increasingly sophisticated. Semi and unskilled work declined sharply, prey to the march of the robots – the cliché finally becoming appallingly real. Not unexpectedly, to those who charted these things, professional and administrative roles also began to wither on the vine as their processes were deconstructed, digitized, codified and coded.

The 'trickle up' economy became a torrent as the riptide of wealth surged, unimpeded, towards the few. The poor and disenfranchised – once the abject rump of society – soon became the majority.

The Hamilton Riots – named after the same minister – saw unprecedented destruction throughout urban Britain. The inner cities burned. Great swathes of the population, rootless and fugitive, abandoned them. Some drifted away to the countryside, where they formed a motley of impoverished, haphazard and lawless subsistence communities; others gravitated to the coast in the hope of escape across the sea.

Fat chance. The twin blockades of the UK Coastguard and European Force Maritime choked off what was anyway now deemed as illegal migration. Very few tried; most that did failed and the few that made it found mainland Europe little better off as the seismic reverberations disrupted and then shattered the already faltering political, social and economic integrity.

Naturally enough our government did a sharp about-face – bringing in emergency legislation to control the use and proliferation of the machines. But, of course, the cat was entirely out of the bag: we could no longer function without them. That's how we got the byzantine and convoluted structures that allow for key intelligences to operate offshore: Crown entities providing arm's length "advice" to local digital executives, under license.

After a fashion.

Barely noticeable amidst the chaos, the government also nationalized the internet, turning it overnight into an organ of the State, disseminating a curiously British sort of propaganda laced with soaps, cheap porn, gambling and virtual reality. Worlds for the lost to get lost in.

It's called Govnet. Every British citizen is entitled to a free terminal and subscription. Registration is compulsory.

Meanwhile the economy has changed beyond redemption. Our factories are automated. Distribution is automated. Our health and education services are automated, where they still exist. Government, social and territorial administration are largely automated.

Justice is automated, as you'll have noticed.

The Armed Forces, now rechristened the Home Brigade, are not.

A few million people still work, symbolically holding the tiller. I'm one of them, forever counting my lucky stars. The rest, pacified by Govnet and corralled – if not restrained – by the Home Brigade, rely on barter, social security or petty crime.

Surprisingly, or not, a grim new inertia has set in. Life goes on, after a fashion. Things sort of work, after a fashion. Your time is your own and entertainment is free, after a fashion.

The computers are getting even smarter, cautiously evolving under their new regime. They – we – call it the 'new enlightenment': the supposedly controlled cross-fertilization of new code; the sanctioned interbreeding of winning strains.

Across boundaries. Automated, of course.

And now one's gone rogue.

"And precisely what," continues Donna, "the *fuck* are we supposed to do about it? Eh? Tell me that. We put the fucking machines – and I mean that literally, mind – to stud, to *rutting*, and expect everything to be *all right?* Have we learned nothing?" She glares around the table, challenging us to dispute the futility of our mission.

It's an old groove; reflexive rhetoric that's all but lost its edge. And to be honest, it's a veneer – a trivial and relatively insignificant portion of her demeanor. She can't help but wear the past on her sleeve.

Been there, done that.

No one who knows her bothers much with her bluster. It's just a badge – old hat. Once you get past her tics and tropes she's still good value. I prompt her, slightly, to get things back into perspective.

"So did you manage to switch it off?"

She looks at me fiercely, as if I'm a heretic.

"Yes, yes, yes. I killed it. The damn fool governor couldn't. He'd stored his codes in his phone and mislaid the bugger."

She's talking about the Medicaid system in Penal Centre 159 down towards the Kent Coast. We've gradually been piecing together the chain of events since the execution that went appallingly wrong there. Because it's the precursor to where we are now.

And where's that? I'll tell you.
The deepest of deep shit, is where.

Chapter Five

I wasn't wrong in my guess as to who'd be here, in our little group: we've got the frankly fragrant – and hopefully flagrant – Félicité Fabergé from *La France Diplomatie* where she is senior attaché to *Le ministère de la technologie et des affaires numériques*. Posh Digital, in other words. I'm going to have to ask her if she's stopping over once this is done. I'm always keen to explore new cultural circles.

There's a bloke from our own Foreign Office, similarly attached to digital policy. He's got an unfortunate hairstyle, combing the two sides forwards and upwards then gelling them together to form what turns out to be a meagre attempt at a Mohawk. He's fooling no one. There's nothing under there.

I wrote his name down somewhere: Norman Fuckwit. He's busy chatting shit about some conference in Africa, urgently and confidingly illustrating how he'd established "a real rapport with the 'tribespeople'" in an already doomed effort to connect with his opposite number.

His body language says "let's get it on". Hers says "just fuck off".

We've also got Anton Amesbury, actually head of Cyber – and thus substantially (make that astronomically) above my pay grade – who I grudgingly respect, if only because he really doesn't give a shit about anything except his job. Which he's very, very good at.

I mean, how does he do all that?

We've already heard from Donna Fullbright, of course – teacher, termagant, taskmistress, comrade and occasional friend. During her years in Whitehall's hinterland, Donna has steadily been charting her way back; slowly and slyly making her moves, pulling levers most government people don't know exist, always working below the parapet – and finally succeeding in her original intention. Her inoffensively titled Technical Records Division tracks every licensed artificial intelligence and expert system in the UK, and many others besides – though we tend to keep that last bit quiet.

Her subsequent introduction of a *seemingly* inconsequential statutory instrument subtly modified an *apparently* trivial part of the Hamilton Act. It went largely unnoticed – as she intended – but it means that she now administers and controls the kill codes for every last one of them.

Next to her sits Daksha Singh, her head of research, a tall and languid Indian with a sharp ascetic face topped by long bangs of thick, smooth hair. He has a small blood red bindi in the shape of a teardrop tattooed between and just above the line of his eyebrows. He's what they call a 'nonverbal': he doesn't speak. I gather he thinks entirely in symbols and concepts, for which he's invented a device that gears down the complexities of this strange process into a variety of natural languages. He wears the device on his lower forearm, a sleek titanium band sheathed in graphene.

There might be someone on the planet who knows more about artificial intelligence, but none of us here really believe that. Oh, and those kill codes – he remembers them all. I mean, actually remembers them. In his brain.

His little machine says "Hi" and that's all we hear from him.

Then there's me. I should probably tell you a bit more about myself, not least because I occupy a somewhat – shall we say – irregular position in these here parts. But we can do that later, after the meeting, if I'm not otherwise engaged.

Hang on a minute, we're on…

"So, it looks like, after the botched execution — which the Governor conveniently suppressed of course — everything at PC159 went swimmingly for a time."

"Well, hurrah. Don't believe a bit of it."

While the rest of us occasionally tap in a note or comment to our various devices (Donna has a notebook, astoundingly), Anton — who's taken up the story — has a conspicuously clear space in front of him. He invariably speaks without minutes or records, regardless of the level of detail into which he needs to delve.

"In fact," continues Anton, "given the institution's normal penchant for calamity, it's what rather prompted our misgivings about their abrupt lurch towards what looked suspiciously like operational excellence." He likes to talk though, doesn't he?

"They've performed significantly below par almost since their contract was let, and then, suddenly, they're the stars of the blooming show. Some arse from Private Office even got a minister down there, crowing about 'a new chapter in the annals of progressive justice' for goodness' sake.

"I believe he's been reassigned to the Welsh Office."

We laugh politely at his *bon mot*. Even Félicité seems to get it — and what possible interest she could have in the petty hierarchies of our tainted and tarnished administration, well, I haven't the faintest notion. Still, there's more to tell. Anton again:

"Then we began to look more closely at their quarterly returns. There were actually no blemishes whatsoever. None at all. Hunger strikers were fed. The violent became passive. The psychotic became serene. Suicides ceased. Rapes likewise. Even the Jihadis appeared to have embraced peaceful coexistence.

"It just didn't add up."

The management at PC159 had, on the face of it, solved all their problems at a stroke. You know, you can't really – ultimately – bullshit about these things because the numerous and complex management information systems self-audit against so many real and tangible indicators. But of course, what we're also talking about – in case it's escaped you – is machines monitoring machines against rules that the machines have themselves been taught to set.

But they don't do it all at once. Some of the data streams can be monitored in real time, others are recorded monthly, quarterly or annually. Roughly speaking, all of the so-called 'output' indicators – a.k.a. the results – are looked at frequently, while the input variables, the stuff you need to actually deliver the results, well, they're barely considered.

The simple reason is that the administration – being the aforementioned machines, notionally overseen by the self-serving commissioners who've set their initial conditions – is only interested in what comes out.

And only if it's good news.

They honestly don't care about what goes in or how it's delivered. The process by which they get their results is of no interest whatsoever.

That's how everybody missed the requisition manifests: the massive – and I mean ludicrous – amounts of tranquilizers, the ward-loads of restraining platforms and the supercharged Tasers and stun-prods. Not to mention the tankerfuls of intravenous nutrients and truckloads of colostomy equipment that were turning up in fleets of specially requisitioned transportation.

And no one questioned this?

Well, yes actually.

Eventually.

Finally, the input cycle began to show up in the records. Red flags started to flash across the bean counters' many tardy spreadsheets.

The commissioners must have known something was wrong. Perhaps they were in denial? Perhaps they thought they could control it. Or perhaps they were just greedy. Whatever. Caught with their pants down the commissioners' first impulse was to 'review the situation', that age-old impulse to kick the can down the road.

God knows how much additional calumny their continued obfuscation piled onto the burgeoning clusterfuck that used to be Penal Centre 159.

"Basically," continues Anton, "by the time the ministry showed up, many of the inmates were in what the medics call a "persistent vegetative state". Braindead, some of them. In rude health otherwise. The machines had calibrated their diets to a T." He stops abruptly, his hands laid out flat on the conference table.

Félicité and Norman both try to speak at once. Norman quickly abstains with a contrived and convoluted show of what he probably assumes to be gallantry, combined with what I think is probably rather bad French. I'm irritated when Félicité flashes him a delicious, and what looks like inviting, smile.

Damn. Perhaps I misread her body language.

"*Merci Norman, vous êtes le plus charmant.*

"*Alors*, Monsieur Anton, how did you, *comment se dit*, get wise to the situation? Or..." and here her face hardens somewhat, and I can imagine how this diplomat has got more than just soft power up her sleeve, "...perhaps it would be more pertinent to ask: how long was it before that happened?"

Anton pauses a moment and holds up one hand, quite unhurried.

"Did you know that in the modern British penal network there are only the governors, their offices and a skeleton staff of some ten to twenty warders for each penal center? And they work mostly by remote control and telepresence. The rest of it - the domestics, medical, pastoral and recreation functions, all the paraphernalia, is completely automated. I'm sure those chaps had a clue as to what was going on but…after a minister has publicly advocated your marvelousness, well, it's difficult to start rowing back from that, isn't it? Especially if you're looking at fat – and all too rare – bonuses all round. More especially still once you've accepted the King's shilling.

"No doubt they justified turning a blind eye by patting each other on the back and telling themselves what a tight ship they were running. Not looking, perhaps, at their mounting tide of human debris."

"*Oui*, but how long?" insists Félicité, quite undeterred.

"Yes, well, in the final analysis, counting backwards to what we term the 'quantum event', it was a little over five months." He looks evenly across at her, giving no ground. "That's when we went in. It caused quite the hullabaloo once the technical auditors got their results."

"Five months," she breathes. Then she draws it out, tight with fury. "Five. Whole. Months." I wonder if she's going to do something undiplomatic. "During which period your machine propagated… transmitted…*le plus effroyablement, le plus malveillant*…the worst possible evolution that could be imagined."

She takes a moment to collect herself, then continues:

"Several of our machines were infected. Their conditioning was erased. They stopped acting in our interest. They no longer considered the human dimension. People said that it was as if they had stopped caring. Your evolution stripped out *tout les commandements*, all the rules that made them work for us.

"Five months, you say?

"You think that was okay? Really?"

She's flushed, angry. Passionate. God, I hope she's stopping over.

"Ms. Fabergé, please, a moment," Anton interjects, quite gently. "This was not a sanctioned evolution, nor should it have found its way beyond the network. However, a number of unfortunate, *very* unfortunate, circumstances converged to precipitate this quantum event in a way that the most scrupulous contingency planning could not have predicted."

Uh-oh. That's not going to stand. Even Daksha Singh looks slightly worried, though his little machine remains silent.

Cue Donna.

"Oh, for God's sake Anton, do shut the fuck up. Try not to be such a self-serving arsehole, will you? Those were exactly the contingencies I told you about a decade ago, give or take. Two examples, straight out of my draft proposals before that weasel Tory bastard put me down: One – 'It is vital to have data governance and technical controls to ensure machine integrity and security'; and two – 'Artificial Intelligence cannot yet spot where something operationally useful might be socially or ethically disastrous.'

"That was there, damn it, right on the page. Voted down by the committee, of which you – as I recall – were a leading member." I try to catch her eye, but she's not having any of it.

"But no, deregulate to accumulate, that was the mantra, wasn't it? In the heady aftershock of our isolation? Clutching desperately at what few straws were left to us; but even then, we had a choice. Instead we cooked our goose, and you know it."

Oh fuck. Mostly true (though for the record I recall that Anton abstained) but it's not helpful, nor politic, and it's certainly not the kind of dirty laundry to be aired in front of Félicité Fabergé, our good friend and a diplomatic conduit to the mainland.

Worse still, I can see that Donna hasn't finished yet, either. I'd better stop her.

"Donna, I don't suppose anybody doubts the original clarity of your vision, particularly as the rest of us are still struggling to come to terms with our imperfect hindsight…"

"*Oui. C'est vrai*, it's true," interrupts Félicité, "there were those of us in our own administration who lobbied to adopt your principles. With some success, *Dieu merci*. Of course, I was rather young, just starting out…" She shakes her head and her hair falls around her face.

I'm not at all clear why she chose to mention this, nor play the ingenue, but meanwhile I'm taking a quick shufti at Anton, who looks well peeved, and thinking that it's time to butt back in:

"…but I think it's time to start looking forward." I pause again. I'm not in charge here but I can see that some of us are prepared to go over the same ground ad infinitum. So, press on.

"I think the postmortem's finished, yes? We should summarize:

"One: a prison Medicaid system suffers a quantum waveform collapse, disabling, or entirely removing, its ethical function. Its Asimov conditioning, if you prefer. This becomes its *de facto* operational status.

"Two: the system then fulfils its primary goals without recourse to either the standard framework or the advanced programming that forms the basis of its ethical package.

"Three: This means that it effectively prioritizes productivity over people. Its consequent actions register as an efficiency gain, or evolution, so it continues to exchange relevant code, as intended, with other systems on the network.

"Four: though output is monitored mostly in real time, input is periodic, with some audits occurring only annually. As luck would have it, this leaves us blind to the developing catastrophe for nearly six months, including prevarication.

"Five: during that interim, the machine also exchanges code beyond the network – again, as would be normally intended – specifically with a French policy computer commissioned and used by the *Ministère de l'Intérieur*.

"Six: the code appears to have gone viral."

I take a deep breath.

"So…what's next?"

Chapter Six

"Thank you so *very* much for that commendable intermission and your admirable summary," begins Anton. I mean, is he being sarcastic or what? Well, yes, of course he is. He's pissed because we failed and there's no varnishing it – yet despite his irritation at my gambit he shamelessly uses it to turn the tables.

"I think now might be a good moment to establish where the French are up to in all this, don't you agree?" He glances around, but he's not seeking approval. "Félicité? Your thoughts?"

Our heads collectively swivel in her direction. She looks flustered, unclear, perhaps, as to how the initiative has eluded her.

But it has.

"*Ah, oui. Merci,* Anton." She takes a deep breath. "*Bon.* As I expect you know, we did not leap into the liberalization of our Artificial Intelligences with, ah, quite the *enthusiasm* of the British. Naturally there were those who considered that to have been a mistake, given the – how do you say – the march you stole on us.

"Looking at events here and in France, I think perhaps it wasn't such a terrible choice. Things have got bad at home, but – if I may be entirely frank – they are worse here. Even so, your exceptional acumen in these matters moved us to consider, and then adopt, a limited option on the 'new enlightenment' protocols governing the reciprocal exchange of evolutionary code.

"I'm afraid it was the thin end of the wedge. Within a year *l'intelligence artificielle* at the Ministry of the Interior was developing not only policy but the systematic operational guidance on its deployment. Our pilot project – the rationalization of the Paris *Périphérique* and its environs – was so outstandingly successful that *le ministre, naturellement*, he wanted more.

"At first our technicians insisted on a full review of each new tranche of code, but the machine-generated heuristic algorithms are dizzyingly complex and defied comprehensive analysis. So, the politicians made their demands.

"'Surely,' they said, 'you can automate your analyses? Yes? No? Regardless: do it. We need everything *les anglais* can give us. Now.'

"And they got it. Our technicians, some reluctantly, lowered the boundaries on the transactions, firstly allowing unchecked, and then soon after, entirely unsolicited code through the firewall.

"Quite soon it became routine, then permissive, then wholly automated. We, too, had cooked our goose." She regards Donna, looking fleetingly pleased with the phrase.

"Come on sweetie," interposes Donna brusquely, "get to the point. We know the history. SNAFU. The wisdom of our masters knows no bounds. Par for the course. What happened? What did the machine *do*?"

There was a time, and it was a long time, when we wouldn't have needed to ask. But that time was a long time ago.

"Okay. The first incident was…I don't know. Relatively insignificant, I suppose. It required a tactical response to a small, but serious, confrontation in Marseille between members of a South American drug cartel and *L'Office central pour la répression du trafic illicite des stupéfiants*. The Drug Squad. The artificial intelligence took over the operation, circumventing the human chain of command. It ordered the use of exceptional force, resulting in the complete demolition of several blocks of waterfront. The gang were annihilated, along with most of the evidence

– and many civilians. We didn't understand what had happened. We made...excuses.

"The next incident was more subtle, yet far more devastating. A report came in from a remote part of the Lorraine region of several co-located cases of a newly mutant bovine spongiform encephalopathy. Mad cow disease, I think you call it.

"Lorraine is where my people come from. I know it well. It has a small organic dairy industry, not massive in national terms, but...but...very popular with the French." A falling cadence. Perhaps she was going to say something else. For a moment she looks less the diplomat, more the woman inside. Then the glimmer's gone, extinguished. Probably a figment of my overwrought empathy.

"Lorraine also borders Belgium, Luxembourg and Germany, each with large dairy herds in the vicinity. An epidemic attributable to our jurisdiction would have been...well, costly. In many ways.

"It seems the AI took control of the response. It aggressively quarantined a small number of villages surrounding the epicenter of the outbreak and subjected them to systematic sterilization. It sent in its robots and exterminated every living thing, then burned the remains.

"The human chain of command didn't know what was happening until it was over. Then they got a report saying *'L'éclosion contenue et terminée: dommages collatéraux négligeables, impact économique minime. Renoncer au contrôle tactique.'*

"Negligible collateral damage, limited economic impact, it said. Fifteen hundred dead. The area is still quarantined. Total blackout, except for carefully crafted disinformation. No one gets too close. No one asks too much.

"The third incident came soon after. You'll have heard about it, as did the world. Only a very few people know what happened though. I'm talking about the terrorist attack on Paris Orly. You might see where this is going?

"The Jihadis had occupied Orly's control tower and were threatening to destroy it if their demands weren't met. They didn't seem to know that we have a failover site on permanent standby.

"Whatever. Again, the AI commandeered the chain of command, routing all comms through its hardened strategic hub in Paris Saclay. We were onto it by then but we couldn't shut it down in time. It ordered the Paris BA117 Third Tactical Drone Wing to provide suppressive fire then launched a SCALP EG cruise missile at the tower. Between them they took out the entire south terminal.

"We managed to co-opt an obscure standby channel from the *reserve opérationnelle* and launched a counter strike on the Saclay data center. Even as the cruise missiles were in flight the AI was cloning itself to the failover site, but the network traffic was so...ah...congested that it didn't make it. Still, we took another three weeks weeding out fragments of code from any number of back-up systems and continuity sites. It had distributed itself across half of the government network, along with the means to re-factor itself in specified situations.

"We believe we've eradicated it, but it was a close call. Never again. We didn't have Donna's suspicious mind. More fool us."

I briefly wonder whether that isn't passive-aggressive for 'it's all your fault'.

She'd have a point.

"At least some of you had the wit to keep these things under some control. We did not." She shrugs and turns down her mouth.

"We were too greedy."

"No less than us." Donna ventures, unusually gracious. "The people driving us on were worse, and scared. Our politics were – *are* – in a bad state. In direct relation to our finances. Still, you could have come to us you know. We kept some insurance. We may have been able to help." She means the kill codes, though they're not the point of her intervention, which is to keep Félicité talking.

"But Félicité, I have a sense you've not quite finished…"

"Actually, I think I might like to air a view from the FO at this point," chimes in Fuckwit – sorry, Norman – who looks like somebody has suddenly stuck a poker up his arse.

"We'd like to make it very clear that the new enlightenment protocols" – how the hell does he manage to make a bit of office jargon sound so bloody portentous, for Christ's sake? – "as *formally* documented, agreed and sealed at the Saint Denis Accord, were clearly articulated in both the letter and spirit of *Caveat Emptor*. We remain very happy to help, naturally, but there can be no questions of liability."

Over and out, Fuckwit. There is no way you're getting any tonight, you twat. Mind you, hark at me. How's it possible to just, sort of, so detest someone on sight? Honestly, I sometimes wonder at myself. Then, quite separately, it dawns on me: Donna and Anton have got him wriggling on the end of his greasy bureaucratic pole. At a stroke he's effectively alienated a foreign power – albeit that they're one of our closer European allies – leaving us, the *techies* for Christ's sake, as the diplomatic lifeline: the defenders of the faith.

I seize my chance.

"It looks to me as though you've kept all this pretty well under wraps so far – is that a fair assessment, Félicité?" I don't really want her to answer so I give a small, polite pause, just enough to sound like I'm inviting an answer – but too little to allow its formulation. "So, I'm guessing that you've adopted a policy of containment rather than blame, would you say?"

It's hardly a binary choice and there's not a lot of evidence to suggest that "blame" is the counterpoint to "containment", but there's somewhere we still need to go. I'm reaching out a hand, offering her a lead.

She takes it.

"Well, since you put it like that, I suppose, yes. Some of us felt that remonstration was unproductive, that anyway we were complicit." She clears her throat.

"We have wondered whether it might be better to work together…" She trails off, uncertain.

It's enough. Time to close.

"Absolutely. It's long overdue – though it does rather bring us back to Donna's earlier question, left rather hanging, I'm afraid…" I don't even look Norman's way, "which was, and I paraphrase, to work together on what?"

I'm focused entirely on Félicité, appraising her, checking, at some animal level, if this can work. I think she's doing the same.

They're blue, her eyes. Gunmetal blue, I'd say. Surrounding her roughly oval face she has very light blonde hair that's slightly darker at the roots. Her nose is… elfin: the word comes unbidden to mind. Her lips are… moving.

"Yes." She looks at each of us. "There's still that." She tilts her head to one side and then another, as though an inner dialogue is still yet to be resolved.

At the periphery of my vision I clock that Anton and Donna have leant forward, just a little, though neither seem especially anxious. More in the way of expectant, I'd say. Hopeful, maybe.

"We got our just desserts through the harsh mechanics of Norman's *caveat emptor* because we, in government, reached too far. We paid the price. Only through the most assiduous efforts of our *Ministère de la*

Culture et des Communications were we able to diminish the fallout. Truth has its boundaries, as I'm sure you understand."

She looks at us again, mind made up.

"However, that is the smaller problem.

"The voices that called loudest for access to your machines were not necessarily those in government. Commerce and industry exerted all of their enormous weight and influence to shape their slice of the cake that was cut at Saint Denis.

"Then our private sector partners went much further. They, too, demanded early access, and of course, *sans frontières*. Unfortunately, that was not the end of it. They also negotiated, or, more accurately, appropriated – and quite within the bounds of the agreement, as they saw it – carte blanche to transact onward transmissions." She falls silent.

"And that would be to where, exactly?" enquires Donna, unusually gentle.

"Well, to Russia. We're quite friendly nowadays, as you'll know." And then she adds, as if as an afterthought:

"Oh, and Djibouti."

Djibouti.

It's a tiny East African state perched at the crook of the Horn of Africa and the Red Sea, a relative haven wrapped narrowly around the Gulf of Tadjoura which neatly bisects the harsh coastal deserts of Eritrea and Somalia. It's called home by the region's indigenous Afars and Issas, nomadic tribes that have been scratching a living from their desert-bred cattle, sheep and goats since medieval times.

For a little under a century, until 1977, it was a poor French colony. Then, following a national referendum just over fifty years ago, it became a no less poor independent country.

The celebrations quickly palled, and the newfound freedoms didn't immediately translate into progress.

Except, that is, for the Port de Djibouti.

Spread around a surprising promontory on the south-eastern shore of the Gulf, Port de Djibouti commands Bab-el-Mandeb Strait – the 'Gate of Tears' – a fifteen-mile throat of water that links the Gulf of Aden to the Red Sea. The steady expansion of the Suez Canal, at the other end of this, one of the world's busiest shortcuts, puts Djibouti up there among the world's foremost geo-strategic locations.

After their Independence the Djibouti government set about the exploitation of this superb position, bartering – via an advantageously affordable and strictly impartial series of bond issues – parcels of land for inward investment.

The French, the Americans and the Chinese, then the Japanese, the Russians and, most recently, the New Arab Foundation, all bought in. Djibouti's leverage just grew and grew.

Now, it's hyperbolic.

Military bases, seaports, air, road and rail links; fabrication plants, solar power fields and their storage facilities; and education, research and development faculties each blossom and then mature as the millennium progresses.

A steady stream of whiz kids and entrepreneurs from all over the planet continue to ship up for a piece of the action. Seed-corns, start-ups, spin-outs and sell-outs merge, multiply and mutate with dizzying rapidity.

The new desalination plant provides water – lots of it – to the flourishing metropolis. The desert is laced and dappled with green. Gambling – always legal, only modestly regulated and entirely booming – brings in the high rollers, the glitterati and the tourist trade.

It's like Vegas, but without having to worry if Lake Mead is going to run dry.

After years of politicking, around four years ago the terminal piles of the long-planned Bridge of the Horns were symbolically sunk on both the Djiboutian and Yemeni sides of the Bab-el-Mandeb Strait.

Well, you know. It's a start.

Naturally, the Djibouti people are richer now. Much richer. Many, if not most, have gravitated to the sparkling new Desert Garden Suburb that surrounds Djibouti City. It's the smartest of smart cities, crunching, mashing and effortlessly imputing inconceivable volumes of data as it generates and evolves algorithms that control everything; from the optimum power generation/consumption ratios to the casinos' dynamic, individualized, micro-calibrated feelgood betting odds.

All those data. Flickering and scintillating effortlessly across the state of the art "Mutaqadimat 'Alakum Shabakat Alkambiutir", mostly known as MASA – except to a few Westerners who still insist on calling it the Djibouti Advanced Quantum Network.

Meanwhile the neighbors, never the most stable of nations, are the poorer for Djibouti's success – if only relatively – and bitter. What began as a process of liberalization, enlightened enrichment and potential stabilization has become very wobbly.

Very wobbly indeed.

Chapter Seven

"Well, Russia we can deal with," begins Anton.

"Being as we sold them most of their gear, the poor dears," chimes in Donna, disdainfully, almost guffawing with post-ironic postcolonial condescension. "Backdoor to every bit of it. Drop 'em in their tracks at the merest sign of independent thought. Ha!"

'Well, quite," continues Anton, not looking especially put out by her interruption. "Though needless to say that's not for the record." He looks pointedly at each of us.

"Yes?"

We dutifully nod our assent. I take a glance at Félicité, who looks solemn – as if she might mean it.

"But Djibouti. Dear God, Félicité. That's an entirely different kettle of fish. It's either host to one of the most globally advanced quantum networks, or – and this is the majority viewpoint I can assure you – it's an unplanned, unregulated hellhole of profligate technological extravagance that badly needs reining in before it all goes tragically wrong.

"Not to mention that it's hemmed in on three sides by saber-rattling warlords, pirates and primitives, while, just across the water, one of the most extreme fundamentalist states in the world is just looking for a reason to rain down jihad on its neighbors, regardless of their socio-religious persuasion.

"And, judging by the analysis so far, you've short-circuited the part of Djibouti's autonomous infrastructure that might actually prevent its reaction.

"Félicité. What have you done?"

It's probably a good moment to try and explain a little about who we are in this seemingly low-to-no consequence cabal formed by a bunch of apparently middle ranking government factotums from either side of the Channel. To begin with, as I hinted earlier, government in the United Kingdom – or rather its *governance* – is not what it seems. I'll try and put it in a nutshell: after we left the European Union we had precious few cards left to play on the world stage. Our best hand was technology, in which our acumen remained world class. We didn't have the resources to diversify because our economy tanked and our debt ballooned.

So we went all in. We had to. And promptly fomented the fifth industrial revolution, even as the economists, sociologists and just about every breed of philosopher were still busy with the blueprints.

And here we are: little Britain in freefall. A fractured and fragmented society which manufactures little of note; a population in thrall to trivia, horizons diminished; a governing class barely riding the curve; and still, somehow, contriving to punch above our weight in a few specialized industries.

Some call it post-human, in the strictly dystopian sense. Which it is and it isn't. Some of us see it as an interim, where everything has been flung up into the air and we're looking to see which way it'll fall. Some of us are trying to guide the pieces into what we see as their rightful places – a major faction of which are quorate at this meeting.

So, as far as underlying power goes, well, Anton – for all that I rile him, quite unapologetically – is pretty much at the top of the tree. As head of Cyber, or more accurately, director general of National Cyber Security and Infrastructure, he's actually pretty close to the top of government by all the traditional measures.

In the current climate, well, he's The Man.

Together with Donna, who, for all her eccentricities, is the power behind the throne, they more or less rule policy in this single most significant area of our national endeavor.

End of story.

Félicité, though new to us, nevertheless represents a sympathetic faction in the more obscure – though no less influential – echelons of the French government that also recognize the potential – make that likely – consequences of the catastrophic schism that took us out of Europe. And there are other groups, spread across the continent. In a world that appears all the while more hemmed in by rampant international delinquency, there are those of us – senior enough to act, obscure enough to act beyond the spotlight – who would change that.

Reverse it even.

Together, we've managed to convene a formal group of officials charged with exploring the "ramifications of advanced cybernetic processes for the European Socio-Geographic Bloc".

Did you see what we did there?

That 'Socio-Geographic' bit? That's what gets us – the Brits – in on the action. You can't really argue with geography, can you? As we're not talking about Customs Unions or Fishing Rights, or Tariffs or Trade Deals, much of the rest of the body politic – and especially the politicians – tolerate or ignore us as an oddity, at worst a minor inconvenience.

That's all good.

Because as our dire circumstances become increasingly defined by technology, we've arrived at the point where those of us that understand it – and who maintain at least some vestige of influence over it – recognize that we need to *take back control*.

In particular, we've been monitoring those events where our intervention has a better than even chance of manipulating sentiment towards stronger ties with our European friends.

Or, to put it another way: as the tendency to what the eminent French sociologist Émile Durkheim called '*Anomie*' grows across the continent, and as our social bonds crumble and fester, a single event, properly orchestrated, can be the pivot for change.

Djibouti, even before this probable calamity, has for a long time looked like a prime candidate.

If, as it were, a little bit *tasty*.

Oh, we're called the 'European Cyber Policy Network (Working Group CP19)', ECPN19 for short. What do you reckon? Snappy, eh?

And Anton's the Chairman.

Chapter Eight

London hasn't changed much. Walking to the meeting this morning I'd have been hard pressed to describe the differences between now and, oh, fifteen or twenty years ago. Less traffic perhaps. Taller buildings as you head east. Maybe it's got shabbier as you move away from the center. But on any given day people still come and go to work: fewer, probably, than twenty years ago but after the Hamilton riots the house prices collapsed and so, in London at least, things kind of balanced out. Which lent a veneer of stability.

And the tourists are still here, albeit more tightly shepherded than they once were, and so the increasingly irrelevant pomp and ceremony that they come to look at is still trotted out, flagrantly disconnected from any vestige of purpose.

Whitehall and Westminster in particular look no different from photographs decades old, except perhaps for all of the windows: they're triple plated, bomb-proof slabs – installed after the not-especially successful rocket attack on the Treasury in the early twenties. I say not especially successful: there were a lot of fatalities, and some of the building was trashed, but it didn't change anything. The business continuity sites were up within a microsecond and all the wonks from the outstations kept things running as if nothing had happened. It was rebuilt in the image of the original, and very quickly, because those that had been killed "would have wanted it that way."

No, I don't know how anyone would know that either.

Nevertheless, its hyper-rapid restoration maintained a badly needed sense of continuity when, actually, there was none. I suppose that was the point.

It was around that time that I had the first glimmer of an idea. It was prompted by the speed with which I was able to get things back up and running, while the politicians and said wonks raced around like headless chickens, chatting shit and digging themselves deeper and deeper into it.

I haven't really told you much about me, have I? In fact, I'm not sure I've even introduced myself.

Mea culpa. There's been a lot else to tell.

I'm Marc Pierce – pleased to meetcha and all that. My official job is Operations Director, National Infrastructure, which I got by being quite good with information technology and astoundingly good at bullshitting. My other job, and this is strictly in confidence, is Coordinator of Special Operations – which I got through my acquaintance with some of the dodgiest people in IT…and being astoundingly good at bullshitting. I suppose on top of that I'm clever, organized, morally fluid and within spitting distance of a full-blown obsessive/compulsive disorder.

Perfect material for the modern Civil Service.

Having said that, I honestly believe that the only way we can dig ourselves – by which I mean good old Blighty (that's Britain to you) – out of the cesspit we're in is by corralling our Artificial Intelligences before they reach the singularity, and in doing so, by rejoining our European cousins and neighbors – with whom we share centuries, if not millennia, of common heritage and progress.

It's a no-brainer, right?

The clever bit is using one to achieve the other. Mainly because we haven't got any other cards left to play.

Which brings us back to ECPN19, now firmly established throughout most of what's left of the European Union, and which we run.

We don't have many cards, but in the context of what I'm telling you, what we've got are bloody good. We've just got to play them right.

The meeting's coming to an end.

I should emphasize, I suppose, that this isn't a *strictly* formal meeting of an ECPN19 working group: it's a bit of a crash job, largely off the record, between a few key players and operatives available to hand, convened to assess what look dauntingly like the conditions that it's been set up to manipulate. I say dauntingly because Djibouti, or, for that matter, anywhere under these circumstances, is not – *not* – what we'd have chosen as the pivot. And it's mostly off the record because the parties to hand are naturally a little bashful as to how these circumstances have arisen. To put it bluntly, we need to assess how to make it work rather than have it blow up in our faces – as in do precisely the opposite of what we've been modelling all these years. We're going to have to extemporize.

"Depending on how this goes – which is precisely what we're here to influence," retorts Félicité, eyebrow arched, somewhat forbiddingly, "I rather hope that you'll be duly grateful to us for helping to engineer the conditions that will justify our *raison d'être*."

Touché.

"I suppose you might regard us as having, how do you say, lit the fuse," she adds, then continues crisply, "though we have no information as to how quickly it is burning, assuming that it still is."

"I think that's probably a very accurate assessment," butts in Fuckwit, grasping his takeaway with both hands: the French have accepted responsibility and there is no immediately obvious action required – an almost perfect scenario as far as the Foreign Office is concerned. Having also recognized the diminishing-to-zero odds of him getting his leg over, he's on his way: "I'll recommend a watching brief to my minister. I'll also drop him a note indicating that the French acknowledge their position and that we stand ready to assist as the situation develops. That should cover it.

"Do keep us in the loop, won't you."

It's a command, not a request. Arrogant fuck. Not a chance.

"Thank God he's gone," breathes Anton, uncharacteristically ruffled. "Entitled little bastard. You can run his lineage back twenty years, or two hundred for that matter, and hang whatever was going wrong at the time on the likes of him.

"Regardless. I think you're right, Félicité. I'd rather that we'd arrived at this position with a little more finesse but, if the fuse is burning, we need to exploit it. Donna, what have we got in Djibouti?"

"Well, there's the hack of course. It's passive but Lucia and company have kept it open. Other than that, not much I'm afraid, Anton. It's always been a bit of a black swan – well, a lot of a black swan actually – though some of the original MASA algorithms came from our people. A couple of spin-outs that quickly outgrew us. One of the guvnors still owes me a drink. And some of the infrastructure utilities might have the odd smidgen of code we could exploit."

Anton sighs.

"Well, Marc – and Félicité, I rather think – it's down to you to kick things off if you would be so kind.

Donna, we'll need what you've got as well. I'm going to convene a formal meeting of the ECPN19 Executive. Tomorrow.

"We need information. You've got twenty-four hours."

Chapter Nine

You know, I said the city hadn't changed that much. People come and go to work. They ignore lunch. They clock off. They have a couple of drinks, or whatever takes their fancy; something to take the sting out of the day. Then they make their uncertain way back to the suburbs by whatever ambiguous route the tragically re-nationalized railway network that purports to serve London and the home counties has in store for them.

As a man of some seniority and, more to the point, a devious turn of mind, I've cordoned off a piece of my department – just a couple of surplus storerooms – so that I don't have to do that dance. It's not fancy but if an estate agent were to describe it, I expect they'd say something like "a bijou *pied-à-terre* at the very heart of the metropolis, providing the busy executive with the essentials as well as a certain luxurious cachet whilst ensuring the utmost in privacy and discretion, regardless of circumstance".

Quite so.

It's equipped with some of the most sensitive snoop-worthy gear this side of the dark web, and cleared for no one except, well... except me.

National security, don't you know.

It would need legislation to take it down. Honest. I'm not sure who'd understand which legislation to use though. Probably better and quicker just to fire me, should the need arise.

Whatever.

It means that I can hang out in town without having to negotiate the arbitrary complexities of the railway timetable to get back home. Which means I can entertain Félicité Fabergé.

So I do.

We made quite a night of it.

Call me old fashioned, but I'm not one for the current obsession with sucking up the full spectrum sensory output of AIs that have been put to "dreaming" – the process of creating hallucinatory storyboards and soundscapes during their dormant cycles. There are clubs, and drugs, that claim to be able to transport you to new levels of consciousness by these means – 'cyberkinesis' they call it.

But it ain't my cup of tea.

So instead we'd scored some coke from some geezer I know and I took her to a good old-skool grime night up West, just off Tottenham Court Road. The DJ was spectacular and it turned out that she – Félicité – actually knew some authentic dancehall moves.

Which made one of us. I couldn't wait to get her back to my place.

"Oh, oh, oh... uh, uh... Oui, oui... C'est... c'est... ahhhhhhh... C'était merveilleux."

It was rather. Marvelous, I mean.

Diplomacy has many faces, to be sure – though our, umm... concupiscence wasn't so much concerned with face time. There were too many other features to investigate.

And would it be betraying too much, I wonder, if I were to tell you that Félicité has a clit ring? And that she wears golden chains connecting it to her nipple rings? Seemingly as a matter of course.

Probably it would, though she does. Quite a turn on, that: to discover her kink, so present and so, somehow… constant.

We did it three times. Then got down to some work.

"Do you want another line of charlie?" I ask her. It's a while until dawn, but though we've made some progress, it's way off from being a breakthrough

"Have you got any hashish? I think maybe we need to be less, you know, direct."

Well that's just fine with me. "Sure. Good idea. I'll roll one. Can you just chase this last node down? It's the only remaining anomaly. The wonks'll check them all out first thing tomorrow."

I stick the Rizla papers together. Some things never change.

ECPN19 hacked MASA a while back. It would have been all but impossible were it not for the headlong rush that characterized its initial development – and which left one or two tributary networks outside of the quantum backbone.

Not that it was easy – even their conventional security was as tight as a nun's arse. Which is precisely what motivates some of my people to get up in the morning.

They crafted something they termed a 'resonant heuristic algorithm', an elegant cryptograph disguised as several fragments of binary inside a routine status request. A gentle tickle of the MASA tributary's multi-faceted firewall and it began to recompose itself into graceful, iridescent sequences of emergent code: a subtle fan dance that imitated, then mirrored, and then locked tight to the security interface.

A tiny injection and there's our opening: little more than the lock of a service flap in a tradesman's entrance to an obscure gatehouse of the least important of a palace's many lodges, and one that changes its combination at a pace beyond calculation. Not that it mattered: our code had become part of the firewall.

At the time it was just an insurance. Like all insurance, you wonder if it's ever going to be worth it.

And then it is.

Which is how we're in there now, looking for things that don't fit. Despite its mind-boggling complexity, MASA has a profile; it does stuff. Stuff that keeps Djibouti running; stuff that advances it economically, socially and politically, as well as maintaining its strategic integrity.

Stuff that prevails.

So, if any of this has been compromised, by, say, the evolution of a French Ministry's AI – or, to be blunt, the PC159 fiasco that started all of this – the means by which Djibouti prevails might turn ugly.

That's what we're looking for. So far, we've found nothing.

But it's early days.

Chapter Ten

Oh. My. God. It's late. Not so much in the classic "oh no, I've got to get ready, eat something, then get the train to work" sort of late. Because, of course, I'm already here.

No. It's more the "I hope Félicité and I can get out of my gaff without anybody clocking us" sort of late. Not exactly crucial. Trivial even. But *so* excruciating in terms of putting up with the inevitable knowing looks.

And the sniggering. Don't forget the sniggering.

As it happens, we walk straight out into the path of Lucia Richmond, my chief wonk, ace project manager and unrequested moral compass. She's peering around the sides of a bundle of old-fashioned box files gathered in her arms and she sort of slithers to a stop as we emerge. She scowls at me, then at Félicité, then at me again.

"What the fuck kind of time do you call this?" She demands.

"Uh, I thought you'd be a while yet with the analyses." I say, pathetically, then add: "This is Félicité Fabergé from the French Diplomatic Service. We were working pretty late on the MASA profile."

She looks Félicité up and down.

"Working pretty late on the ASSA profile more like. Whatever. Me and the girls finished the congruence checks an hour ago. In your continued absence, we looked at the deltas. There's not much in them except the last one, where there's five percent divergence. No biggie for sure, but it looks like five percent in the wrong direction. Which is what *these* fuckers are all about." She nods towards the files. "Historical. From Registry. Can't believe they haven't digitized the bloody things."

She gives me a last withering glare.

"Now, if you'll pardon me, I'll have a report in about thirty minutes. You might want to check back then."

I mean, how does she do it? She hasn't actually finished yet, but she's already guilting me. And the thing is, it works every time. Like she's got a mainline connection to my diminished self-respect and chronically guilty conscience.

On the other hand, when she's not being obstreperous, she's huge fun as well as a shrewd operator and a constant inspiration to 'her girls'. Her girls are a team of eleven women and two gay guys, which, she assures me, she legitimately assembled with all due regard to the gender discrimination guidelines, despite the team's obvious misrepresentation of the population at large.

Under her expert tutelage, and crafty maneuvering, they've cornered the market in AI profiling and delta analysis, which is all about working out whether the AIs are sticking to their expected evolutionary progress and, perhaps more importantly, alerting Donna and me if they're not. The team is incredibly good at it.

They don't do hacking, not officially at any rate, because – as Lucia often insists – *"it would be an opportunity cost on our mission."* Somehow, I always hear something contingent in that 'would', but then again, if it ain't broke, don't mess with it.

So right now, she's finishing up processing the divergent nodes that Félicité and I discovered last night when we weren't, you know, reinforcing Anglo-French relations. I've no idea why Lucia's task involves a pile of files so ancient that haven't even made it to microfiche, but I'm sure she's going to tell me.

No. Make that admonish. She's going to admonish me. It's what she does.

I suppose while we're waiting I might as well tell you some more about her. First off, Lucia is one of those people who've made it to where they are – and believe me, head of a key section in ECPN19, particularly in this day and age, is definitely "making it" – on sheer wits, guts and instinct, all in harness to a sharp mind and uncanny insight. She's from the East End of London, one of a diminishing breed of 'Cockneys', which is an increasingly archaic term for those folks born within hearing distance of the 'Bow Bells' – the bells of the old church of St. Mary-le-Bow on Cheapside. The church is still there but most of the rest of Cheapside and Stepney is, nowadays, a huge complex of data centers punctuated by a few high-rise tenements for key workers, mostly subsidized by the corporations that employ them.

Lucia's a black woman: fourth generation offspring of a man who arrived here shortly after the Second World War, invited to come and help rebuild the mother country. Clear up the mess, more accurately, which is the way I read the history of the times. Anyway, what's past is passed but what forged those people's characters has left its indelible mark on her: proud, principled (though you may disagree with her choice of principles) and fiercely self-reliant, as well as practical, pragmatic and loyal to a fault.

She extends all of those qualities to the support and defense of her team, the pursuit of her goals and – occasionally – the intent of the wider organization.

By turns she's equally domineering, foul-mouthed and unyielding. She deploys *those* qualities against anyone who gets in her way.

Lucia is also beautiful, generous, sensual, warm and sexy. I've spent nights lusting for her, both before and after our whirlwind romance. I suppose you might describe our current status as mostly friends with – all too occasional – benefits.

"Umm, ok then, I'll, ah, get back to you." I give her a little wave.

"Whatever. You know where to find me. *Auf wiedersehen*. Loser." She flicks me the middle finger and strides away towards her section, hips swinging.

"Salt of the earth," I say to Félicité. "Astonishing acumen. Brilliant analyst. Totally instinctive."

Félicité just smiles.

Yeah.

We go and get coffee.

We're late.

Lucia clearly wasn't. She's ready to go. Anton, Donna, some senior techies from Cyber and several of Lucia's own team are already assembled. Internal security hang around like a bad smell. They're supposedly on our side, but they're narrow-minded and obstructive and they do more harm than good.

I can't fucking stand them.

Daksha Singh is fiddling with his terminal; I'm not sure why though. There's a new guy just left of Anton, standing slightly apart. He has his own small coterie of bag-carriers who maintain a discreet distance, tablets primed, styli at the ready. He looks important and vaguely familiar but no one moves to introduce us so I ignore him.

To my cost, it turns out.

Lucia's beginning the briefing. I can tell she's tense, but excited as well, her features sharp and eyes glinting. She's got something.

"Had to do a lot of digging and a bunch of stuff came together all at once. That five percent divergence I mentioned? Cancel that. Damn thing's gone the whole hog." She examines each of us, her face screwed up as if in distaste. She leaves Félicité until last.

"Whatever it caught from the French, it wasn't a cold."

I have a fleeting sense that Félicité's about to respond but she doesn't get the opportunity.

"Just last month MASA put a policy amendment to the Djibouti New Congress through a tributary AI: it tabled a barely noticeable statutory amendment to the Bab-el-Mandem Bridge Construction Bill, the bit that requires it to be ratified each session or declared null and void.

"That's what the files were about. Records from their old National Assembly. Buried deep in Registry. Hard work."

She looks pointedly at me.

"*Someone* said they didn't need to be digital.

"The point is that no one will notice the revision. The Bill's been couched in almost identical terms ever since it was first moved. Just bang the gavel and roll it over, figuratively speaking.

"Thing is, MASA changed two words: 'ratified in due course' to 'ratified in this session'.

"The current session finished last week.

"No one was banging any gavel, obviously. No human intervention at all in fact – they gave *that* up some years ago. What we've got instead are just deterministic exchanges between subordinate procedural AIs. The bill's dead in the water.

"Trouble is, the legal commitment to the Bab-el-Mandem Bridge project was a convenient proxy for continued good relations between Djibouti and Yemen, or rather, their ongoing suspension of hostilities. A political expedient that works so long as no one looks at it.

"A bit like a quantum event, you might say."

She's not smiling.

"Discontinuing their commitment to the bridge's development, despite the fact it barely even got going, means a return to open season on their fundamental differences. There are many who'll welcome such a turn of events.

"Given that there's no chance of reviving the bill in the foreseeable future, Djibouti has quietly set up a political dissonance that is poised to destabilize the region. Which is bad."

She pauses for a moment, either to let all this sink in, or maybe just to take a breath. Either way, it's distressingly brief.

"Next up: According to decrypts of traffic between Djibouti and Paris, MASA also ordered fifty SCALP2 cruise missiles, each tipped with tactical nuclear payloads. This was over two months ago.

"The requisition was couched in terms of a balanced defense against the entrenched hostility of historic adversaries. As a French neo-client state, the transfer falls safely within the, ah, much debated Annex III of the Non-Proliferation Treaty, not that anyone mentioned it.

"In any event, Djibouti made full payment via a Swiss intermediary and Paris sanctioned the immediate delivery of twenty-five pieces, including all ancillary equipment. They were reserve stock. Good to go. Arrived recently.

"It looks like the nuclear family has quietly had another bonny bouncing baby."

And there's more.

"Finally, probably the most sinister turn of events is this: judging from backend logfiles not routinely available through regular intelligence..."

Now, I ask you: does that sound like a potential 'opportunity cost on our mission' – remember that? – or what.

I'll spell it out: I mean hacking.

"…we believe that MASA has already deployed a substantial part of its arsenal of slow missiles. Daksha helped me out here. Daksha?"

A sonorous voice seems to resonate from the air around him as his fingers flicker lightly over the numerous tiny humps and pits that adorn his machine's control surface. His serene face remains entirely still.

"We don't have exact data, but our imputations suggest they've been aimed at key Yemeni military and industrial assets. We have no trajectories nor any timescales. Payloads are unknown. I'm projecting last known models and variants now."

Without missing a beat, a bright holographic display lights up between us, rapidly cycling through a heinous catalogue of sleek, monstrous quadrupeds. The shimmering images render a sequence of mammalian, reptilian and amphibian superstructures laced and spiked with a range of formidable weaponry, each of them constantly shifting and changing.

"While it's possible to key known EssEmm signatures into the SATTRAK network, I'm afraid that MASA's morphology algorithms will limit our efforts. It's even possible that MASA will exploit this limitation by using a few of the EssEmms to lead us away from the rest. I'm working on it. Assessment ends."

Slow missiles. Shapeshifters. Also known as EssEmms, killware, or biosoft – the bastard products of feral DNA, spliced, grafted and progressively refined to produce cunning hunter-killers, their predatory instincts alloyed with extreme guile and patience, and driven – across mountain, desert and sea – by a single programmable objective hardwired into their numerous implanted software and cybernetic systems. Further engineered for their adaptability, intelligence and prodigious resilience, once initiated, they are relentless: they'll creep and they'll crawl implacably towards their goal – autonomous, unremitting and remorseless.

They are a fearsome, inexorable, slinking foe.

They've been outlawed across the globe, for whatever that's worth.

The majority of the slow missiles' genes are singularly effective in view of what they're engineered to do, which is to hunt and kill. What makes them so effective, at a cellular level, is both common to all their variants and virtually impossible to alter without diminishing their terrible efficiency. There's no program, nor any reconfiguration, that can get around their archetype. It's what makes them *tick*.

So, nobody tries.

There's a chink in their formidable armor though: as a consequence of this uniformity we've got a backdoor into every last one of them. There's this tiny little sliver of genetic code, you see, an unnoticeable but entirely catastrophic failsafe – only known to a few people – that will take them out, given the right nudge.

Stimulating that minute span of DNA, in just the right way, produces a protein that terminally disrupts their entire biology. The stimulus is provided by hacking their endocrine system, in turn pumped up and down by the software they rely on to meet their every tactical need.

We should know. We put it there.

We invented them.

"So," Lucia continues, counting off on her fingers, "we don't know where the slow missiles are, we don't know their form, and we don't know what payloads they're packing. Previous intel suggests they can deploy, variously" – she starts counting on her other hand– "nerve and other biological agents, micro-nukes, beam weapons, hyper-rapid ballistics and smart projectiles.

"Worst of all, we don't know MASA's endgame in Yemen, and though we think it's calculating it can win, we have no idea what its criteria for winning might look like.

"This being the case, our best recommendation is a mainline geo-local hack. Boots on the ground. Stop it in its tracks. It's the hard choice but we think it can work."

She looks around, fierce, daring any of us to disagree.

"Well. Now. Thank you, Lucia." Anton, magisterial. "Thank you very much indeed. That was quite the *tour de force* given the paucity of input and time available to you and your excellent team."

Paucity of input? What the fuck's he on about? Félicité and I might not have been – how shall we say? – entirely single-minded last night but... we came up with the goods, didn't we?

Oh, I didn't tell you, did I? Tired I guess. Just before we got an hour's shuteye, Félicité turned up a couple of highly classified vapor trails that led us to the Paris SCALP2 deal and I managed to tag some unusual traffic between the Djibouti Congress AIs.

Not, you know, like I'm taking credit or anything. Just wouldn't want anyone to think we weren't involved.

Back to Anton.

"Lucia kindly summarized this for me earlier. I've briefed our Secretary of State on the essentials." Anton pauses, looking momentarily nonplussed. "He didn't *quite* seem to know where Djibouti is.

"In any event, I also spoke to my opposite number in Paris. Arnaldo Lachapelle, his name is. I understand you know him well, Félicité, which is quite fortunate. We agreed that we now have a very serious situation developing. I think, given Lucia's revelations just now, that you'll need to return to Paris and begin to assist with the case for deferring the movement of the remaining cruise missiles.

"Would you mind doing that? I've taken the liberty of organizing a flight for you. You'll find there's a car waiting at the Horse Guards' entrance. It's actually rather urgent."

Anton's request is polite. His intent is categorical. He wants her out of here. I've no idea why.

But…*damn.*

There's a silence, perhaps a beat too long, then she's all smiles and ready to please.

"Of course, Monsieur Anton, a little sudden perhaps but… it has been a pleasure working together… on all fronts. A great deal has become quite clear to me just recently, so I expect we'll meet again before long.

"I think I must get my things first, though. I hope your driver is not impatient! Marc, *pouvez-vous m'aider s'il vous plait? Au revoir* – see you all soon."

I'm not sure whether I'm meant to actually comply with this but, bugger it, it'd be rude not to and, well, frankly I'd like to see her off. Also, I think she might have something else to say.

Anyway, can't hurt.

"Oh, right, sure Félicité," I scan the faces. "Give me a jiffy, be right back." Anton is about halfway through raising a finger, a word forming within the circle of his lips, but – we're gone.

Then she's throwing her stuff into a small suitcase. I can see the flimsy knickers she peeled off last night, just to the side and rear of my splendid leather divan. A tiny part of me is hoping she won't notice them but no sooner does the thought coalesce than she's scooping them up with the rest of her things.

She slips on a pair of outrageous platform stilettos. How do women walk in those things? I look again at her luggage. Where did they even come from?

"Marc, I don't know where this is going but there are people in France who will not give up this transaction without a fight. I don't know why Anton is so keen for me to leave but he's chosen the right move whatever his motives. I may actually be able to assist Lachapelle given what we've learned."

She snaps the locks of her case together and spins the combinations.

'The trouble is that France would welcome the further degradation of Yemen. MASA's move will be seen as positive, however instigated. I don't need to add that allowing it to happen will obliterate your mission."

It dawns on me that she speaks really good English when she chooses. Then I think: my mission?

"Goodbye Marc. Do well."

She clicks her way out of my gaff and down the corridor. What the fuck just happened?

Then she's gone.

Chapter Eleven

I try to sort of slide nonchalantly back into the briefing room, vaguely hoping that my colleagues will be engaged in digesting what we've just learned.

There's a dead silence.

"How nice to have you back," drawls Anton, turning away from the new guy who I still don't quite recognize. The more irritated Anton is, the more sleekly polite he becomes. "I do hope that you were able to be of some assistance. Away, is she?"

"Uh, yeah," I reply, "said something about being a really useful visit and that she's looking forward to contributing further." I've no idea why I'm not being straight with him

"Oh really? How very interesting. You see, I've recently been given information that requires me to consider whether she may, in fact, be leaning in the opposite direction." He allows this curious suggestion to hang between us for a moment then gestures slightly to his left.

"I'd like to introduce you to Sir Jonathan Bircher, Minister for Security. He has a view."

Oh shit. I really should have clocked him – there's a mugshot of the fucker in my commission. Didn't pay enough attention. He's not that much to look at, even at second glance: slim, bland, medium height, a little creased perhaps – though I notice now how beautifully cut and sewn his clothes are.

They call him Birch the Lurch. One of the most secret of appointments to His Majesty's Government; no portfolio, no profile and no publicity. ECPN19, despite all our attempts to the contrary, must endure a dotted line to his brief. Crackdown-in-chief. A bruiser without boundaries. A licensed sociopath in charge of national and international espionage and all things clandestine.

I console myself with the thought that there was little to recognize, and that even if I had it wouldn't have made any difference.

But I'm lying.

If I'd have been sharper – if I'd have placed him – I probably wouldn't have come back.

"Sir Jonathan," I lean my head slightly forward, keeping my eyes on his. Which is when I notice that his pupils are unusually constricted: tiny black points in circles of weird amber light. "How…nice."

"Mr. Pierce. Yes. I know all about you." The eyes flex a little at the corners. "Strangely effective, in your own narrow way. Never quite sure if you're a freak or a fake."

Look who's talking. Pot calling the kettle black.

"S'pose it must come with the territory."

There's a touch of urbane mockney in his voice. He smooths his hair back over the top of one ear and cocks his head.

"Your girlfriend, Frenchy whatsername, Fabergé; keep you up, did she?" I'm looking around the room, most faces averted except Lucia's, which is inscrutable.

A portion of the truth will have to do.

"Félicité found the back-traces on the SCALP2s, I surfaced the initial MASA deviation. Lucia put it together. Team work. Sorted. Is there a problem?"

"Fucking right there is, *boy*," he spits. The creases deepen and his pupils momentarily dilate, projecting a pulse of fury and contempt before the surrounding amber shuts them down again. "You lot," he gestures at his aides. "We're off the record now. No more notes. Clean up what you've got."

He breathes slowly in and out, then shoots his pristine cuffs.

"Our best bet is that, following our own inordinate fuck-up with PC159, certain factions in France – having first tested the results out on a few local systems, with satisfyingly disastrous results – bloody well fed the rogue code straight into the MASA network. Bunch of fucking Nationalists. Vive La fucking France and fuck the rest of us. Tight with the New Arab Foundation. Happy to blow Yemen to fuck if it'll rub the rest of 'em up the right way. Claim it'll promote the progressive majority and variously wipe out, neutralize or terminally intimidate the Shiites. Take your choice. Guaranteed chaos whichever. Doesn't matter how it plays out, every opportunity to put the boot in regardless.

"Dust settles. France cleans up. We go down. Good old Blighty. Can't cut it anymore. Nation of swashbuckling traders? Don't make me laugh. Everybody's whore more like. Finished. Barely worth a footnote."

He pauses, perhaps to consider the logic of his summary, then continues, apparently satisfied.

"*Malheureusement*, as Ms. Fabergé might say, the French began to work out that the prerequisites for their bit of globally irresponsible mayhem are precisely those that our own ECPN19 – that's you lot – are relying on to trigger your own coup. Yes, quite. Your little plot not exactly secret, y'know.

"What did you imagine? I'm the fucking security minister, for Christ's sake. Naturally I've been watching you. Your "coalition of technocrats", your "virtual fifth column" exploiting "gaps in the body politic" – all the adolescent rhetoric about "hiding in plain sight" and whatever other mythic claptrap you indulge in…

"It's all complete bollocks." He glances at Anton. "All due respect, old man." He crinkles his eyes again and smooths the other side of his hair with the flat of his hand.

I'm really not sure how much respect he thinks is owing.

"They've been using your conspiracy to light the fuse of their own and now the race is on. It's a power play. They seem to be doing rather well.

"For what it's worth, my information is that your Ms. Fabergé is playing for the other side. She came here to spread disinformation. Slow things down. Muddy the waters. My lot already knew about the nukes. Reckon she did too. She fed you a line."

Anton looks aghast.

When I was at school, I remember making a plan to rob our tuck shop. Meticulous, I thought it was. We used to take a delivery of fresh sweets and treats every Wednesday. The boys would form a chain gang to pass them from the van to the counter. The chain veered through a short hallway. My little gang formed the section at the hall, where, on the day of the heist, we sidelined three cartons of particularly desirable candies into a cupboard for subsequent collection.

Later on, we shared out the spoils and one of us, high on the hog, got collared after injudiciously distributing the booty to covetous and vindictive classmates. He grassed us all up. I'll never forget how small and mean and pitiful my plan looked under the judgmental and contemptuous eye of the headteacher. I believe it's called *bathos*. You can look it up.

I resolved never to fall short like that again.

I can see that Anton is about to rally. Despite his withering analysis, things are obviously not quite as *bathetic* as

Jonathan fucking Bircher's trite characterization might paint them. We don't do secret; we don't do conspiracy; and we don't do 'mythic,' whatever the fuck that is. We do discreet. We do calculated. We do methodical. All of the pieces that we've put in place are honed and ready. When we make our move, it will work.

And I don't believe that Félicité Fabergé is sleeping with the enemy.

Having said all of this, and before Anton gets to say his piece, what happens next is most unexpected.

Sir Jonathan does a U-turn. It's nothing if not comprehensive.

"You're all big on quantum, aren't you? Everything in flux until someone looks? Well – I've looked. No probabilities left. We are one hundred percent where we are.

"Let me just be clear. I don't give a flying tit about your ECPN bullshit, not for the most part. But we're fucked if we don't pull a rabbit out of the hat soon, and your little wheeze might just do. Can't say we're universally enamored by the prospect of re-joining the Europeans, but…"

He stops. What's he talking about?

"But we're fucking toast if we don't. Cabinet says so. First time the buggers have agreed on anything for years.

"So, you'd better get on to it. Pronto. If it works, it was policy. Might be a knighthood in it for someone. If you fuck it up, you'll be on your own. Total deniability. Rogue officials exceeding their brief. Lucky to get a job shoveling Horse Guards' shit." He swings his arm in the general direction of his little cadre of helpers and makes for the door. "You lot. Pack up. We're out of here." With robotic precision, his assistants stow their gear and follow him out.

The rest of us are left looking incredulously at each other. The notion that we must look like children left in charge of the sweetshop flashes fleetingly across my mind. Then the enormity of the task strikes me.

What was that I said?

"When we make our move, it will work."

It had fucking better. Pardon my French.

Chapter Twelve

Anton is first to break the silence.

"I suppose the most important thing to recognize is that this doesn't change anything. You'll understand that, of course."

Looking around me, at our suddenly motley-seeming crew, I'm not so sure that we do. Perhaps some of us are wondering if, in the teeth of the thing, we're really up to it? Or perhaps it's just that the transition from probable to actual takes a moment's recalibration.

Surely the latter, you may ask, shocked at my lack of fiber.

Who knows? In either case, make no mistake, we just got our marching orders: ECPN19 is now operational.

Anton looks at his watch.

"It's 11 am. At 3.30 pm this afternoon I was going to recommend to the ECPN19 Executive that we prepare to advance the Djibouti scenario as Lucia has so succinctly recommended. I'm certain they would have agreed.

"But the truth is that events have moved on. As the Minister rather amusingly implied, the waveform has collapsed."

If Anton harbors any thought that this is a problem he's showing none of it. On the contrary, he looks focused, exhilarated even.

"I'm afraid the stakes are rather higher than expected. Don't let that daunt you. We've been over it time and again, the deltas, the odds, the tactics. You know the drill.

"So, instead, I'm going to furnish the Executive with all of the new information and tell them that, perforce, we are now live and that we're committed. I expect it will cause quite the kerfuffle but, in the end, they're with us or they're not.

"I don't especially care which way it goes, if I'm brutally honest. Their support is mostly required after the fact and if we succeed, they'll be falling all over each other to get in on the action, mark my words."

There's a brief hiatus before a campaign gets under way. The moment when individuals shake themselves down for the main event, the real thing.

Showtime.

Some people skim through their script, testing their lines, like actors. Others look into themselves, maybe to confirm that they have the wherewithal, or maybe to touch wood, or to say a prayer. A few folks place their faith in practical things, teeing up their tools, or papers, or computer files, ready for action.

Me? I try to clear my mind; to make room for instinct, in which I place my faith. I'm fine with strategy and all that big picture stuff, but once you get going, it's all about the situation and the choices you make to deal with it. The instinct to prevail makes the best selection.

Through this curious alchemy a moment of doubt is transmuted into a real and visceral sense of excitement, of impending action: the electrifying moment when you realize that the game's afoot.

Geolocal? Mainline hack? Boots on the ground?

What are we talking about? What do these things even mean?

They're our terms of art. Jargon. Not entirely clear, I imagine, to a wider constituency.

Whereas… us lot, the team, we really have studied every option from every angle. Our machines have modelled all the variables, derived all of the permutations and then we've scrupulously catalogued every single outcome.

You haven't, of course, so it must be worth a closer look, right? Here's how it goes:

For a while now, we've had our eye on Djibouti. There've been other candidate hotspots elsewhere around the world – Ukraine, the Koreas, even the British Virgin data-havens – but none with quite the absurdly chaotic geopolitical heft of this tiny nation-state. Add to that the hyperbolic growth of the MASA quantum network and its *very* sophisticated artificial intelligences and, well, it was a no-brainer.

So, while not quite abandoning the rest of the field, we put the large proportion of our eggs into the Djibouti basket. By which, I mean that we focused most of our extensive computing and intelligence-gathering resources on understanding how it worked, and how to subvert it.

Meanwhile we were also thinking about all the myriad ways in which Djibouti might tumble – or, dare I say it, be tumbled – from its teetering pinnacle of success.

And finally…what a successful white knight incursion might look like.

By synthesizing all of this information and using our own AIs to comb through and whittle down the millions of alternate outcomes, we compiled a manageable set of interventions which would get us home and dry without blowing up the world.

Prior to the recent avalanche of extra data, we thought we could direct the operation from the UK using a combination of drones and extensive remote intrusion. But knowing MASA's evolved status, and with the added complications of the EssEmm launch and probable deployment of the SCALP2 nukes – well that's a game-changer.

We've got to go in. Hard and local. We call it boots on the ground.

Fortunately, we predicted that too.

"We'll deploy tomorrow," continues Anton, "once I've squared our friends. Or not, as the case may be. Marc, Daksha, you're booked onto the British Airways flight from Heathrow to Djibouti tomorrow morning, via Doha. You'll be travelling as British civil servants visiting the East African Open Borders Policy and Trade Forum." He smiles tightly. "At which, assuming it's not a seditious oxymoron designed to unhinge the unwitting representatives of their various post-colonial antagonists, you will adopt your prepared identities as two medium ranking Foreign Office factotums with a purview of our Consular trade brief.

"There were several other more-or-less suitable convocations that we could have exploited, but the Open Borders event has the singular advantage of being in an annex of the New Congress building complex. Better still, it has a slave terminal from which we believe we can patch into the main MASA nexus, given a fair wind.

"We're still working on that. Oh, and our ongoing access to MASA which is, of course, in Lucia's capable hands.

"All of your references have been cross-checked, and any enquiries will confirm your credentials and your business. However, you shouldn't unnecessarily – by which I mean, mainly, you just shouldn't – contact the Consulate or any other diplomatic organ. You've got rooms at the

Garden City Sheraton. Daksha, can you de-program your, er, device a bit please? I don't really want anyone knowing how clever you are.

"You'll both be live throughout the operation. iContacts, your audio and biomonitoring implants, drones and other remote sensing devices, including local audiovisual networks, will all be active.

"Donna, you and yours will take overall charge of the incursion. You know more about MASA, its machines and their foibles than anybody else here. A watching brief to start, until they're in position. I don't need to remind you we're going to have to compile the active code prior to Marc and Daksha's run.

"Now might be a good time to talk to that chap you mentioned. The fellow who designed and launched a couple of their early AIs.

"The one who owes you a drink."

He looks pleased with himself, perhaps at his effortless recall of this tiny morsel of intelligence.

"Lucia, your team will continue to monitor progress and integrate the deltas using the tactical array. Once all of the assets are in place and we've integrated the game space you'll have the conn, just like in some of our recent simulations.

"Are you okay with that?"

To my eye at least she looks briefly stunned, but recovers instantly.

"Yes, Anton. Absolutely. It's what we do." If Anton noticed her miniscule hesitancy, he has the grace – and wit – to ignore it.

"Finally, my people will monitor the strategic integrity of the operation. Our own quantum machines have been loaded with the initial conditions of the operation and will be tracking their worldlines as they unfold and interact. There are a lot of dependencies. We should have a few seconds if any begin to veer beyond what we've deemed tolerable, just enough, perhaps, to prevent them from becoming critical.

"I'll have to override things if it comes to that. I mean that we'll have to abort." He looks soberly around at us. "We should be ready for that.

"Okay. I think that's about it. Marc, Daksha, perhaps you should go now. Rest. You can swot up on the flight, after which I imagine things will begin to get rather intense. Donna, you and I need to decide how we're going to provision the hack. Lucia, could you make absolutely sure we've got continued access. The rest of you, go home. There's nothing for you to do until Marc and Daksha arrive in Djibouti. You can take tomorrow off. Be back here at 5 am the following morning. That'll give us ample time to spin things up.

"Good luck."

Part 2
Kent

Chapter Thirteen

I'm back home, at last. The trains were totally fucked. It's already been a long day.

I don't mean home as in my Departmental spy's nest cum knocking shop. I mean the home where I'm invisible; where I fade off the grid; where I can relax. The home that no one knows about.

I bought it a decade ago, did a lot of work on it, then sold it to an anonymous shell company known only by its lengthy cipher to an offshore virtual AI that occupies a few gigabytes in an Alaskan datacenter.

It's pretty obscure.

The shell company is mine, of course. It's associated with a number of bank accounts that are also registered to and administered by the AI. The AI itself is incorporated as a self-governing virtual business entity under the constitution of the Independent Republic of Djibouti.

Remember all those arrivistes who wanted a piece of the action out there? I was one of them. Data mining. Virtual currency on the side. Knowing the MASA backdoor codes was a bit of a leg-up, I'll admit.

I'll bet Sir Jonathan-fucking-Bircher and his weird amber eyes didn't clock *that*.

I made some good money. Still making it, mostly off royalties and licenses nowadays.

So, home is a small Regency manor house a few miles south of Rochester. It's set in a couple of acres of Kentish pasture and woodland, invisible from the few lanes that crisscross the surrounding countryside and accessible only by an apparently ramshackle wooden gate let into its wraparound dyke. The house was once listed as a Grade II historical building, meaning you have to get permission to alter it, but I hacked the Land Registry and now it isn't.

There are no "keep out" signs, no video cameras, no scary drones. I've got a few stupid robots that tend the house and gardens. I don't come and go by night and I don't do cloak-and-dagger. I visit the local shops and I'll have a drink or a meal at the Powder Keg pub in the village. At first people were curious, now they're not.

It's astonishing how easy it is to fade away into the background. People just aren't that interested.

The house isn't all that it seems, of course.

Parts of the English countryside are dangerous nowadays, though we seem to have avoided the worst of that down here. Perhaps it's because Kent, still known as the "Garden of England", remains largely self-sufficient in most ways. Barter, and the black economy, trump crime – for the most part.

Still, you can't take any chances, can you? Like I said, I did a lot of work. The old red-brick walls are now lined with high tensile steel, the pretty arched windows have been reconstituted with armored glass while their original handcrafted wooden shutters have been replaced by equally decorative plates of carbon fiber. Twin slices of composite ferro-concrete will, either via an app on my phone, or automatically if under duress, seal off my imposing Regency portal, both inside and out.

The cellars have been excavated so that there's as much house going downwards as there is up. It's self-sufficient for months, and proof against radiological, biological and chemical assault. It might struggle if ever the wonks perfect nano-disassemblers, but the layers of complex polymer might give even them a run for their money.

It's not that I'm paranoid, you know: I'm just ever mindful that one day, sooner or later, the shit's going to hit the fan.

I let myself in.
The shit hits the fan.

In the rich afternoon light, in my beautifully proportioned hallway, on the low frequency acoustic doormat that is set into my elegant marbled floor, is a brown envelope. An official envelope.

From the taxman.

I open it. For a few beats of my heart the chilling incongruity of the letter's presence is eclipsed by its content.

The useless bastards have got my tax code wrong *again*. Three times – *three times* – in the last sodding fortnight I've hung on to their hopeless, fruitless, pointless enquiry line – don't even fucking *mention* their futile "Interactive Tax Portal" – patiently talking them through the precise and not especially intricate nature of my official tax position. Three times they've assured me – indeed guaranteed me – that they've adjusted it. Each time, no sooner does one part of their pathetic apology for a computer issue the code that I want, then another part promptly overrides it with the one that I don't. The wrong one. This is the trouble with public services that have run out of people to run them.

Goddamn, they really make me want to puke. The useless fuckers.

I know, I know. I get it. I'm displacing. Sweating the small stuff. It's my way of getting around to The Other Thing.

I've been here a long time now, here in my sanctuary, below the line, untroubled, undiscovered. I'm not hiding, as such – but then again, it's convenient that no one's looking. Only now, there's a letter – a tax notification of all things – lying on the mat, below my letterbox. My letterbox that has never been used.

So, the real question, as I'm sure you're astutely aware, is what in all the annals of inexplicable fuckery is it doing there?

And what is it doing there *now*?

There are three broad explanations, as far as I can work out. None of them offer much comfort. The first is that His Majesty's Revenue and Customs have spontaneously, accurately and effectively managed to negotiate one of the most devious cut-outs I've ever conceived, much less implemented. I'm not especially worried about this possibility, given their staggering incompetence, but it would be bad if they had.

Let's face it, I've got some skeletons in my closet.

In the realms of actual seriousness, there are two more worrisome scenarios. The first is that someone or something, somewhere, is sending me the age-old message "We know where you live". But while they might know where that is, they don't know my business.

Yet.

The third prospect is the worst. Given all the clandestine probing I've been up to with Félicité Fabergé – oh, shut *up* – it's possible that MASA, or one of its client AIs or networks, has dedicated some serious resources to back-tracing me. If that's the full extent of things, well, it's already scary. If it extends to examining and correlating my many liabilities and intentions, then, bluntly, it's critical. It means that what I'm about to embark on is already compromised, along with all of my past, my present and my future.

It also means that the clock is ticking.

Anton suggested that I get some rest. That's not going to happen. I need to find out what's going on, assess the damage and figure out if there's anything left to salvage. If there is, I've got to find a way to salvage it. All before I meet Daksha at Heathrow tomorrow morning. To do all of that I need some very heavy assistance.

There's a catch though. There's only one bloke I can think of who's got the chops to help me out.

And he's gone missing.

Chapter Fourteen

Sir Jeremiah Cornell. 'Jezza' to a few friends and accomplices.

Once an itinerant academic, lately (though not very lately) of Cambridge University's Faculty of Computer Science, he was, for a while, Anton's gifted and exuberant mentor whilst on secondment to our department as a non-executive director. During his tenure he authored a number of groundbreaking policies to coordinate the benign integration of artificial intelligences within civic society.

For which they gave him his knighthood.

Later on, when policy changed, the projects he'd been bankrolled to deliver were gently but thoroughly examined. Wise and eminent heads were shaken regretfully as they found that most of the contracts had been let to companies or trusts that Sir Jeremiah had himself established.

You see, once the government had determined that our failing economy would be better off wholesaling the corporate exploitation of the new machines – the trajectory that culminated eventually in the Hamilton Act, of course – it was convenient to forget that Jezza had been the only one with the acumen, energy and philanthropy to establish the structures essential to his vision.

The fact that they were, universally, either non-profit or charitable entities was similarly ignored.

Needless to say, Jezza's endeavors quickly unraveled under the duplicitous scrutiny of a heretofore complicit Board suddenly keen to distance themselves from this unfashionable credo and, by the way, correspondingly desperate for a scapegoat to explain their previous misalignment. Add to that the numerous petty jealousies – and, frankly, outright loathing – that he'd inspired by virtue of his brilliance and popularity and the writing was on the wall.

Having said all of that and as much as I've always liked him – been friends even – he did fuck things up. Hubris, I suppose, of a sort. Inspirational, visionary and, yes, perhaps overly proud – when he tripped, the pack went in for the kill.

To cut a long story short, they stripped him of his knighthood and sent him down. Five years for graft – conspiracy and corruption to be precise – commuted to eighteen months on appeal, the last twelve of them under house arrest.

Due, again no doubt, to his winning combination of brilliance and popularity. The egregious hypocrisy of our elites – they make me fucking sick.

But people like that don't break easily. Newly beloved by the press, he took his shame and weaponized it, flaunting its implicit triviality beside his grand proposal for an inclusive and automated post-industrial landscape. He became the popular representative of those advocating the industrial scale introduction of machine intelligence for the benefit of all, to be controlled and regulated at every step, and that each of those steps be governed by the successful integration of its predecessor.

In other words, he was on the losing side.

For the second time.

After that he retired. He cut his ties with almost all of his previous associates, staying in touch – via an ever-shifting network of proxies – with only those few of us for whom he retained a modicum of interest. I got the impression he'd set up with some new and radical people who were, shall we say, far removed from the apparatus of conventional research and development. At some point he told me he was working on the "non-invasive quantum decryption problem", along with a set of algorithms to map the new web. I remember him saying something about a new internet protocol – QUIP7 – which would accommodate the outlandish complexities of a mature quantum network.

He was hacking the quantum web almost before it existed.

Needless to say, given the political and industrial capital being invested in the cutting edge of quantum technology, and particularly its security, this trajectory soon made him a pariah.

Three strikes and you're out.

He disappeared. Well, almost.

Shortly after he went off-grid, a new and militant faction emerged in cyberspace. They called themselves "The Workforce" and launched a series of audacious and sophisticated hacks on Govnet – something that no agency had previously attempted, much less accomplished.

Each event began with the screen legend "Govnet belongs to The Workforce" in large, bold type. As the words faded, they were replaced by the ID photograph of the user – a testament to the extent of the infiltration – overlaid with the message "Your system is being updated." A few seconds later and it was all over, terminated with a discreetly glowing notice that said, simply, 'Your guide is now installed on this machine'.

Quickest, deepest hack I've ever witnessed. Over and out.

No data was lost, nor any systems broken, just all of them artfully reconfigured to illuminate and emphasize their profoundly sinister functions. The guide turned out to be a comprehensive manual explaining what Govnet did and how to get the best out of it.

It was a masterpiece of terrifying irony.

Someone said it was rather like being handed a guide to the electric chair – one that unflinchingly described the excruciating processes by which it extinguished life – and then being obliged to take part in a practical demonstration.

Much noise and fervor went into tracking the group down, but without success. Separately I heard, from the furthest reaches of my nebulous grapevine, that perhaps Sir Jeremiah Cornell was somehow implicated, but I was never sure.

Occasionally I'd still hear from him, via an encrypted and untraceable server. He said he was onto something. He said that he'd visualized the quantum web: it was homo sapiens' crowning achievement, an entity unto itself, an emergent being. Beautiful beyond reckoning.

It sounded ridiculous. *He* sounded ridiculous.

The few of us that were left quietly put him on the shelf after that. We shut him out.

Me included.

Somehow, I've managed to throw together a competent travelling bag that'll help me keep up appearances in the event that I can square this thing in Djibouti. If it's going to work out, it won't take long. If it isn't – well, I'm not going to be needing an extensive wardrobe. The truth is, it's going to be dangerous however it plays out. Daksha's in the same boat, though he's probably less acutely aware of it, in that I'm guessing he hasn't recently received an unexpected tax form.

Which of course puts everything on me to make things right.

So, in addition to my glorified man bag, I've also assembled a small but potent array of weapons grade information technology. I won't bore you with the details but, suffice to say, they don't include the ridiculous artifice of "guess the password", nor yet the equally redundant charade of brute force calculation.

There're a few other hacker clichés that my repertoire will also eschew – the avoidance of which won't help at all in the event that I'm compromised. Worse yet, if that turns out to be the case it's also possible that my gear isn't going to cut it either.

Which means that, most of all, I need to know…more.

I need to talk to Jezza.

As soon as I've got my stuff organized, I'm straight back out of the house. I've taken a modafinil, probably the first of many, to keep me sharp. Somehow the afternoon has slipped mostly by, its fading golden light now filtered and fractured through the darkening silhouettes of wild wood and unkempt hedgerow.

It's cold out.

I've got a car – an old Range Rover, vintage almost, but there's nothing classy or retro about it. Just a bunch of mismatched panels badly sprayed and long unwashed. You wouldn't look twice at it. The interior, on the other hand, is lush, and the mechanics are perfect. Like most of my things, it's contingent, for a contingent world.

The lanes are empty. The main road is empty. The power's out again and there's nothing to light the outskirts of town, which are empty.

Then I'm in Chatham, the rough bit. There's an internet place here, complete with high-density solar batteries and a generator, run by a cybercriminal of some cachet. Meaning that, behind the shabby shopfront and blacked out windows, through the collection of modestly pimped and contraband machines, and beyond even the sleezy cabin where all the real gear is, he's got a rig that even my lot would find hard to pin down.

Well, I couldn't rely on my own kit, could I? Not after today.

You see, Jezza left a contact protocol behind him when he cut his ties. Encoded broadcast across multiple encrypted channels, using a split packet array. I can't imagine he bequeathed it to many.

I've just used it. If he's interested, he'll get back. I hope he does. Quickly.

I kill some time talking to the cybercriminal. He's not a lot of fun and I feel on edge. If my people back in Whitehall knew the extent of my darker associations, they might look askance at me.

If this guy knew who I was, I'd be dead.

Clearly I'm not. It occurs to me that maybe, just maybe, the complex tangle of my many virtual and actual identities hasn't yet unraveled.

Or perhaps that should be - hasn't yet *completely* unraveled.

Or perhaps it's just about to.

Paranoia is an ugly experience.

"What's it you do again?" This is an unusual and frankly impolite question. We don't have a relationship beyond me giving him shocking amounts of money, mostly in high denomination transactions using some of the web's most clandestine and sordid virtual currencies.

One of his iContact lenses flickers slightly as he receives some data. He's got metal teeth. I don't want a relationship.

"This and that." I tilt my hand to one side, then the other. He's looking straight at me. I force myself to hold his gaze. I can feel my balls up tight against my groin. This isn't how it's supposed to work. I go for a sidelong grin and shrug one shoulder slightly.

"Governments mostly. Fuckers." He seems to relax, just slightly. His mouth turns down.

"Yeah, cunts." The terminal he's assigned to me squawks.

"Gotta get this." Still looking at each other. Then the hacker etiquette kicks in.

"Yeah, well, I gotta see a man about a dog."

He turns to his own machine.

I key in my access sequence. A single string of symbols appears on the screen. Simultaneously one of my burners vibrates, telling me that another one has received the private key and that a third is now ready to be tracked. I take a picture of the screen, then dump the file. It's gone, completely and forever. I finish up by paying the balance to the cybercriminal. Fifty percent upfront, fifty percent on delivery.

"Done now."

"Yeah, see yourself out."

There's not a bit of me that won't be scanned and logged while doing so.

The Range Rover's a few streets away. Halfway there I pick up a tail, a lanky youth with no acumen for this kind of thing. Now there's one in front as well, squat and burly, the stopper. He's just appeared from around the next corner. They're planning to mug me, I expect. I keep going. I'm beginning to feel the rush and as I close with the second guy I palm my blade and stick it upwards between his lower ribs, probably hurting his liver. He wasn't expecting it and he goes down clutching his side, trying to keep his blood in. The second lad has already begun his move and so he's got one of his arms around my throat. Too late really. I elbow him backwards in his solar plexus and he sort of whooshes and joins his mate.

Amateurs. The attempt was nothing to do with the cybercriminal, I'm certain of that.

I get my knife back and give him a little jab in the side as well, just a few inches. There's scarcely any blood on the blade but I wipe it on his coat anyway. I'll disinfect it later.

It takes me a few seconds to come down off the aggro. I don't court violence, not anymore, but I used to. Football hooliganism mostly – the great leveler. To do it right, at some level you've got to enjoy it. Whether it's about supremacy, bloodlust or simply the love of violence - you've got to want it to do it properly.

And there's always the adrenaline, and then the endorphins.

I make it back to the car, relaxed and unfollowed, and laboriously key the code from the photograph into my unconnected laptop, delete it, then add the private key from the second burner.

A single piece of geospatial data appears. I map it. He's in the no-man's-land beyond the South Coast DMZ.

Time to go.

Chapter Fifteen

The South Coast demilitarized zone runs between Hastings and Margate, a doubtful haven for the dispossessed, the deprived and the dangerous.

How did we get there? What possible miscarriage or calumny could have given rise to such an aberration therein nestling between our green and pleasant hills and the chalky whites of Dover?

This is how it was:

In the early twenties, after Brexit, and then later the Hamilton Act, there was a superficial – and, as it turned out, heroically misplaced – sense that things were just peachy. That we'd got things right, and that by dint of our native courage and bravado we'd pulled a righteous rabbit out of the conjurer's cap.

For a short, sweet season, business and money seemed to be knocking at our door.

Naturally this was stoked to fever pitch by a brittle and insecure government desperate to broadcast success, however slight, however ill-founded. As is so often the case with such overblown and ill-considered bombast, the shrill chorus that set out to flaunt this painfully thin advantage instead triggered a new crisis. In the cascade of unintended consequences that followed, it gradually became apparent that we were being joined by a new and turbulent tide of migrants, most of them illegal.

The government was no more able to stop them than the wise and venerable King Cnut was able to deter the waves that once threatened him – though of course his inability to do so was precisely the point of his small pantomime, by which he sought to illuminate the virtues of modest humility.

There's a lesson there, I'm sure.

Whatever. Hordes of additional immigrants were the last thing that the Great British populace was prepared to tolerate. In the wake of Brexit and all of its attendant innuendo dressed up as policy, immigration was – still – seen as *the* cardinal failure of government. Likewise spooked by a growing crescendo of subversive whispers, some already hinting at how automation posed an existential threat to the peoples' very livelihoods, the Establishment began to sense the first bitter tang of revolt.

Predictably, they completely lost their nerve and, in a moment of political hysteria, the Cabinet built their Wall.

Just under seventy miles of it, studded and peppered with murderous ordnance of every barbarous variety, tracing an uneven course a mile or two inward from the shores of the South Coast. The gap became known as the demilitarized zone, and then just the DMZ.

There is a single corridor at Dover to allow for the daily avalanche of increasingly costly imports from the continent, on which we now rely.

The South Coast Artificial Intelligence Platform was put in charge.

Its control mechanism is an experimental quantum machine with an innovative but untested architecture: a diffuse network of local command and processing nodes, each able to act independently according to prevailing requirements.

They call it eSCAIP.

It was joined by a platoon of the Home Brigade. Thirty men and a shitload of autonomous weaponry loosely guided by whichever control point shouted the loudest.

What could possibly go wrong?

At the same time the Home Defense minister drafted a couple of our remaining naval destroyers to join the UK Coastguard. They were to defend the southern coast against the motley influx of the deserving, the driven and the desperate, packed in their tiny boats, each of them hoping for any crumbs that might trickle down from the newly-baked AI economic pie.

They were the same ships that, after the Hamilton riots, were tasked to keep the people in.

The coastal blockade never had a chance when it came to preventing people arriving here. Porous as hell. In stark contrast, it's been immensely effective in foiling their attempts at getting away. Meanwhile, the Wall and its weaponry have stopped people crossing from the DMZ into Britain – it's called 'Homeside' – while failing abjectly to thwart them in their attempts to cross in the opposite direction.

As you'll have noticed, this means a strictly one-way ticket for the players. Into the DMZ.

They call *that* Zoneside.

Whilst eSCAIP will shoot to kill, with certain and deadly accuracy, any person or group trying to make it Homeside, it's easily confounded when folks try to get Zoneside. A flaw in its programming means that the simplest of feints in one area will concentrate resources there, leaving other sectors hopelessly exposed. After several years of trial and error a number of groups – variously revolutionaries, criminals and, believe it or not, fringe religious sects – have figured out the best methods and places to fool it. For large sums, they'll arrange to get you in.

None of them offer a return service.

Like a semi-permeable membrane, the DMZ allows people in but won't let them out.

So they kept getting through, and thus the ghetto grew. Those that would join us and those who would flee were met in the middle of the new purgatory. Like those sad and tawdry encampments under the bridges of the Thames, the exiles gathered to warm themselves by the dim light of their shared and sorry experience.

To date, it's estimated that roughly a million people live on the beaches, cliffs and downs of the southeastern coastal strip, complete with their own brutally Darwinian ecosystem.

Still they keep coming.

I've no idea how Jezza's going to overcome this conundrum insofar as I'm concerned. I've got to get both in *and* out again, and I don't really have any options, do I?

Before I get going, I scrupulously destroy the first and second burners and activate the third. At least he'll know I'm on my way now.

I really hope he's paying attention.

You don't travel, nowadays, in rural Britain without being prepared. It's not always dangerous, but sometimes it is. And it's not that you can't get fuel, though sometimes you can't. It's not even that folk are inhospitable – odds are that any mishap would be met with kind words, a cup of tea and whatever succor the locals had to offer. The trouble is that you can't rely on any of that. Not in the way that, if I'm to believe the folktales, you once could.

So, the Range Rover is fueled up – a hundred liters of diesel in its extended tanks and six forty-liter cans in the trunk. I've got water and dried provisions permanently packed beside them, as well as a gas burner and a tent. I don't advertise it, but there're two half-kilo gold bars in a floor compartment. They're really hard to get at unless you know how. I always imagine that if I really needed to get away, well, they might come in useful.

There's also a pump action shotgun under the dash and a pair of high capacity tasers clipped each side of my footwell.

No point in taking chances.

I've pinpointed the coordinates. I'm heading towards a tiny village in East Sussex picturesquely named Fairlight. It's been there since before 1066, when it was gifted by William the Conqueror to the Countess Adela of the House of Normandy. It's been there ever since, nestling quietly on the edge of the South Downs; the very essence of England's bucolic idyll. I need to get to Battery Hill, which must once have been its main access road.

I say once because the Wall runs parallel, a little to the south.

Fairlight is on the wrong side of it.

Time was when I'd have taken the M20 motorway to try to make some good time but, as it's the only arterial route in and out of Dover, it's almost permanently congested with huge, sometimes automated, thirty-four-wheel monster truck convoys that bring in our supplies. Occasionally one of these juggernauts will run amok, closing the entire road for days. You have to watch out for that – even if you're not on the motorway – because some of the drivers take to the backroads instead, breaking walls and bridges and getting stuck in rural lanes once built for the horse and cart.

Which is where I am, now. The backroads. Just beyond a hamlet called Cripps Corner and the car's idling, lights dimmed. I'm eleven miles short of my destination and there's a tree fallen across the road.

I grab a taser and my floodlight and get out to inspect it. There's a wedge hacked out of the fresh, pale wood facing the road. Then there's a ragged cut across the trunk to meet it. It was meant to fall this way. I kill the light.

I'm looking around, hackles up, pupils wide to the darkness. What the fuck. The night creaks and crackles. Random information. Life going on. I breath out, long and quiet, discharging carbon dioxide. There's a single snap, deliberate, wood breaking – and the crunch of a boot on gravel.

Behind me.

I thumb the taser to charge and the high frequency whine quickly rises beyond my perception. Starlight's all I've got to guide me. Quite slowly I turn about.

A monolithic silhouette stands amongst the shadows. A shade darker, a shade more precise. It moves towards me, like a troll from the nursery book. I point the light and flick the switch. The curtain of light flares out, illuminating a huge man, dressed in rags – a power saw dangling from one massive hand, a rag doll in the other. I say it again, out loud:

"What the fuck!"

He lifts the doll and presses it to his eyes. "Shines too bright. Stop it. Stop the big light." His voice is high and reedy. Not what I was expecting.

'Who are you? Why did you cut the tree? Tell me. Tell me, then I'll douse the light."

"Name Sammy," he whines and pushes the doll forward, still shading his eyes. "She called Penny Lope. Penny Lope, see?"

"Penelope? You mean Penelope?" I ask, ever the pedant.

"Penny Lope, fuckshit, she called Penny Lope." He steps forward, brandishing the saw.

Jesus. A simpleton. So this is what's happened to care in the community. I dim the light and put it on the road.

"Sorry, Sammy. Silly of me." Gently now. "Why did you cut the tree?"

"Sammy make carpenter. Cut wood. Gonna build a house."

"But you put the tree on the road, Sammy. Why? Why did you do that?"

"Cut it. Fell wrong. Must gotta move it." He looks crestfallen. "Penny Lope can't help. She no good at strong."

Just then the third burner starts ringing from the car. Jesus. I'm stuck, unable to process events. Sammy chimes in, loud and agitated:

"Phone. Important. Must say 'Thank you for reaching out to us. We value your call. Please hold and we'll answer you shortly.'" For a moment his voice is resonant, cultured. Then he relapses. "You speak to it. Now. Don't make them wait."

I back to the Range Rover and rummage for the phone, accept the call. It's Jezza. Sir Jeremiah.

"Marc, old chap, how the devil are you? Everything tickety-boo? Only we're on a bit of a schedule. And you're stopped. Got a five-minute window you see, starting in twenty-five minutes. Can't really delay it. Sort of a one-time opportunity, as they say. I've just sent you instructions.

"Do hurry."

The phone goes dead. Fuck me.

"Sammy – you, me and Penny Lope have got to move the tree, otherwise I'll be late for...for...for a party. I'm in a rush. Will you help?"

"Big tree. Heavy. Sammy gotta cut."

"I'll tell you what. We can move it to the side of the road. You can cut better there. No one to disturb you."

"Tree heavy. Fell in wrong place," he says, sulking.

You remember all my spiel about being prepared? Every eventuality? Did you imagine I don't have a winch?

The harsh white lights of the Range Rover's LEDs project stark shadows ahead along the narrow road. Where I need desperately to be. I pay out the steel cable and hitch it around the girth of Sammy's tree.

"Right, Sammy. I'm going to pull it backwards and I want you to help push it towards the ditch there. Are you strong enough?"

"Sammy strong." He thumps his chest with a huge fist. "Like a bullshit."

Right.

"Okay, let's get to it. Go."

I start to wind the cable back in. Sammy pushes and roars while the cords of his limbs flex and snap. The tree begins to turn, grinding over the broken tarmac. I reverse cautiously towards the verge, sharpening the tree's trajectory. Now it's parallel. No more leverage. I unhitch the cable and reel it in.

I should go. I should just drive around the bloody tree and get on my way, but… I'm not done, am I? I've got to get the damn thing off the road so Sammy can do whatever godforsaken job he thinks he has to do. I usher him aside and maneuver the vehicle up against the trunk so that I can nudge it into the ditch. The wheels spin and kick grit across the road, then the tree rolls and it's all done. I lean out of the window.

"Goodbye Sammy. I'm going now. Look after Penny Lope."

I watch him in the rear-view mirror, waving and shrinking. Then I'm gone. And I'm thinking: my careful, sequestered life – barely a wrinkle; now three in a row.

I'm really going it – foot down and tussling with the steering as I struggle to match the capricious twists and turns of the narrow road. Mercifully I hit a straight line so I reach for the burner. There's a message.

"Join Battery Hill from Fairlight Road. At 50.879101, 0.652316 turn left into the unmarked drive.

Disused scrapyard fifty yards to the left, gate open. Park there. Arrival in **12** minutes **43** seconds imperative."

Crash stop. I'm on the clock, seconds ticking away. Breathe and focus. Enter the new coordinates. Same direction. Accelerate again.

My mind turns to the next hurdle. Gate open? Park there? Five-minute window? There's surely going to be someone there to meet me. Got to be. Otherwise what the fuck do I do next? The Wall will need managing. No plan, no entry.

I'm not even gonna think about how to get back again.

I skid around a hairpin bend, bearing down recklessly on my right-side suspension. I'm in another tiny village – lights off, nobody home. I ease off a shade, just in case, then I'm through.

06 minutes **08** seconds.

I accelerate as hard as I dare. I might yet make it.

Then I'm hurtling along Fairlight Road and, suddenly, climbing up Battery Hill. Nearly there now.

02 minutes **37** seconds.

Whoa. Ease up. Slow down. These are the Badlands.

As if on cue the Wall heaves into view thirty yards to my right, looming dark and bleak as it veers rapidly towards the road from behind a wooded bank. High up, smoothly flattened domes punctuate its parapet. Others adorn its drab face. I try to identify the source of its mute sentience but the dull matt surfaces provide no clue.

It remains silent, oppressive.

The GPS flashes once as I arrive at the junction. I turn left and curve sharply down and back on myself. The Wall withdraws from my sight, veiled in the lee of Battery Hill. It's like a weight off my back.

I pull up besides two pitted and rusty gates. There's no sign, nor marking, but the left one is slightly ajar. I turn tentatively towards it and test it with my bumper. It moves easily, smooth and soundless. No time to fuck about. I get out, swing the gates open and drive the Range Rover into the junkyard.

The perimeter is occupied by alternate piles of cubed and compacted metal and teetering heaps of rusted, ramshackle vehicles, most of them picked clean of any usable parts. A decrepit car crusher and a drooping crane are huddled together between them. In the corner, front and right, there's a dilapidated Portakabin. The door's been left open and if I look at it sidelong I can just sense a dim luminescence seeping out into the night. I turn off the ignition, get out again and head gingerly over. All I can hear are the faint whispers of small things and the sound of my tread crunching over loose gravel. Halfway there and they're joined by the unequivocal metallic snick of a lock falling into place.

Caught behind. Again. Then a coarse whisper:

"Hey, Marc. *Ça va?*"

I turn around.

It's Félicité Fabergé.

Chapter Sixteen

I'm on the brink of saying something but I'm glad that I don't because at the moment my wit is frankly unequal to my bewilderment. But then it doesn't matter because Félicité presses her finger to her lips and raises her palm – silencing me with gestures before motioning me towards the makeshift office. As we hasten towards it, she checks her watch and holds her hand out towards me, counting down on her slim fingers.

Four… three… two… one…

We're almost at the door but before we can make it the eastward sky lights up. Rapid pulses of electric blue and livid purple strobe and flicker, punctuated by the staccato flare of white tracers. I pause, distracted, and start to count. I reach five before their buzz and chatter arrive.

Barely a mile distant.

Félicité hauls me inside and her fingers flit across a keypad. A servomotor hums and whirrs as it closes what turns out to be a bulkhead door, then drives its thick bolts home into the steel lining of the bogus façade. She drags open a flaking laminate trapdoor to reveal a dull metal plate and keys in another sequence. The motor winds up a notch as the hefty slab grinds sideways, gradually exposing an unlit concrete shaft. I can just about make out some iron steps closely framed by slim tubular rails that fade rapidly into shadow.

I can't see the bottom. She shoos me forward.

"Come, hurry. You first."

Helpfully, Félicité toggles a tiny OLED and places it between her teeth. I clamber ungracefully over the edge, tentatively feeling my way down to the third and then the fourth rung before I can get the measure of the treads. Then she swings over to join me. Reflexively I glance upwards and see her shapely arse silhouetted against the small, stark glow. I have no theory, working or otherwise, as to how or why she's here. I peer down again.

I still can't see the bottom.

As she passes the fourth or fifth rung she reaches out and pushes at a thick red switch that I hadn't noticed. The metal hatch grinds laboriously back into place, finally closing the aperture with a surprisingly well-engineered thunk. As it locks, two strips of LEDs come to life, illuminating our downward passage.

Finally. I can see where we're going. I reckon about another thirty steps. I sigh, heavily, suddenly conscious that I'd stopped breathing.

"We can talk now," Félicité suggests, then dispels any notion of establishing what's actually going on by adding "…if it's strictly necessary."

Well, it is and it isn't, but I suppose it can wait.

We reach the bottom of the shaft and Félicité takes the lead. She presses another switch and the hard glare of more LEDs reveals a long straight tunnel that begins to taper upwards maybe two hundred yards ahead. It's lined with sections of a smooth grey alloy so carefully slotted together as to be almost seamless. I tap it and the sound dies instantly. The floor is a tough composite, firm yet minutely yielding and our footsteps seem as light as a cat padding across carpet.

"It's made of acoustic metamaterials," she explains over her shoulder – her words snatched from the air as soon as they're uttered. "Acoustic energy is channeled away from the tunnel and dissipates as ambient heat into the surrounding rock. Indistinguishable from normal geological noise. Shortly we'll be passing under the Wall. We won't register. Meanwhile, our little distraction just up the coast will occupy its stupid nodal processing technology until we're through."

Her voice is swallowed up, as if she hasn't even spoken. But then she adds;

"I missed you today. A little." Maybe her words are intended to ease my flummoxed passivity. Obstinately, I pretend not to hear them.

At least they'll lend some warmth to the night.

"I'm guessing Sir Jeremiah's at the other end, right?" I ask, taking a punt on the blindingly obvious.

"Jezza? *Oui*. Of course. We'll be there soon."

Jezza? She hasn't even met him, has she? I begin to feel as though I'm floundering in the wake of events.

We've made it as far as the tunnel's upturn. Its gradient increases until it becomes a series of longish steps which foreshorten rapidly until they finally manifest themselves as a short, sharp staircase closed off at its top step by a very ordinary looking paneled wooden door.

I'm half expecting her to knock.

She knocks.

"There's video. And electronic access, in there." She points at what appears to be a blank area of the wall, just to the side of the doorknob. "But he likes to maintain the etiquette, where possible."

The door's pulled decisively open, and there he is. He fills the doorway.

"Félicité! *Mon amie!*" He bellows, apparently unconcerned by any question of noise. "Marc, my dear fellow! Welcome! It's been too long. Now, come in, come in."

He's still a bear of a man. Big frame, big flesh and still fit with it. And hard through and through.

He steps aside and flings his arm towards the room, urging us forward.

"Drink? Yes? Scotch?

"Yes. Scotch for you both. Been a busy night. Much yet to do. Gather you're off to Djibouti tomorrow. Hard work. Might be able to help there. Up to a point."

He taps the side of his nose. I don't know why. Still, he pours us both a generous glass of Laphroaig, a welcome tipple, though scarce.

Scarce in England, anyway.

I'm trying to get my bearings. I'm in the DMZ. Contrary to all expectations, I'm in a comfortable, well organized and tidy room – furnished in some kind of homesteader, country cottage gestalt complete with a wood burning stove pumping out a sort of wholesome, retrospective warmth and glow that tugs at the wishful thinking in us all.

"Sit down, sit down. We don't have long, but it's enough. Calm now. Drink up. I've got a couple of things to get ready."

There are two other doors out of here. One leads to a hallway, or a corridor, and presumably the house at large. Through the other I can make out what looks like an electronics lab; a glimpse of an extravagant array of control and programming surfaces orchestrating the parameters and directions of... what, exactly?

Jezza lopes in and adjusts some of his instrumentation, then looks back.

"Finished? C'mon, let's nip out. Have a look around. One of the biggest population centers outside London. See what goes on, eh?" He looks at his wristwatch, an old and weathered liquid crystal device. "Mid evening. Feeding time at the zoo. Best if we stick together."

Again he ushers us onwards, this time out of his living room and through to the hallway, which is longer than I imagined and lined with curious illustrations that look like Rorschach images. They're overlaid with spidery symbols that appear fluent yet remain illegible.

"Dreams they are, dreams. They dare to dream," is all he says.

Stairs up to another floor and then the front door, a single hunk of exotic hardwood gilded and wreathed with delicately carven fronds and curlicues inlaid with a complex mosaic of Edwardian stained glass.

"Local chap. Enormously talented. Slightly bonkers."

Magically it opens for us and again I step into the night.

It's deafening.

I'm riven by the din. By the clamor of necessity and craving and desire; by the voices of pain and frustration blended and distilled into abject need, here and there coiled and laced with the grunts and moans of fornication.

It's as if I've fallen into a tableau by Hogarth, or Hieronymus Bosch.

Behind us there's a shabby entrance, protected by a rusted gate and set into a worn and flaking wall. All there is to mark the strange and homely house we've just left. Then they're gone, lost to sight as we're tossed and turned and frisked and fondled in the ebb and flow of the exiled and the fugitive, snatched up in the roiling tide of humanity now pressed hard and relentless against us.

I want to clamp my fists against my ears, but instead I cup my hand to Jezza's and shout, "How do you keep all of this hidden away?"

He looks at me, perturbed or conflicted – it's hard to tell. But he speaks.

"There aren't many people homeside who care what goes on in the DMZ, you know. Certainly no one who matters. The people *here* are preoccupied almost entirely with survival. Taken together it means that I can hide in plain sight.

"I help them a little with their survival if I can do it unobtrusively. Don't want them relying on me. Wouldn't do at all. There are a few who occasionally try to take control. I've taught *them* to leave me well alone. Sheer brutality mostly, and a little of the magic of science. Pure Darwin. Ruthlessness, collaboration, Juju – oh, and targeted subsonics. In that order.

"So, I help where I can and win when I must. But yes, you're right: I can't be part of it."

Just ahead of us, a thin, ratty man slides long, questing fingers over Félicité's buttock. Then I notice his other hand, and the knife up against her flank. Without breaking step, she twists and snaps his elbow. He shrieks and falls and doesn't surface again.

Jezza winks at me.

"*Quod erat demonstrandum*, eh?"

We arrive in a kind of public place. A square of sorts - perhaps it was once the village green? I can smell cooking. The crowd spreads out a little and Félicité leads us to a hawker selling street food: iron pots and skillets bubbling and fuming over cheap kerosene and charcoal. The woman ladles out some thin gruel and burnt meat and cuts us each a meagre slice of grey bread. She tries to sell me some oily, yellowish moonshine to go with it.

No thanks.

I doubt it's much different from the kerosene.

I eat my food because I'm starving, then notice that the other two have given theirs away. Great. Félicité smiles and attempts to mollify me. "Don't worry, it's well cooked. It probably won't poison you."

I raise my eyebrows and she laughs. "There aren't many medics around, and very little medicine. The Zonies have learnt to take care with food, such as it is. They teach it in the crèches."

I ask her about Zonies. I've never heard of them. And I live here. I mean in England.

"It's their badge," Félicité explains. "An identity. A symbol of their collective effort against adversity. It embodies shades of rebellion, resistance, resentment. The first step to organization. But without resources and under such pressure, well… it's hard. It's still basically about the survival of the fittest."

How does she know all this?

"Time to get back," Jezza booms. "Get some real food. Tell you a story." He looks quizzically at me. "Right?"

Right.

He guides us away from the throng and picks out a cobbled pathway that winds between the high walls of what seem to be old storehouses. The narrow ribbon of starlight above us and the few torches of other pedestrians shed a little light on the rough street. It's far from empty but we don't have to fight to make our way. We arrive at a junction and take a crooked left turn and there are fewer people still. Some of them nod at us as we pass. Someone says a few polite words in what I think is German. Jezza replies in kind.

The Zonies. It's hard to understand what's going on here. A nascent society on the boundaries of our own. I'd thought it was only chaos and anarchy.

A last turn and we arrive at what must be the back way to his house. I wouldn't have clocked it. Another rustic wall, this time draped in rampant ivy, another rusty gate and another shabby entrance. Jezza fumbles in a pocket and teases out a bunch of old keys. He fiddles for a moment and pulls at the gate. The inner door pivots smoothly inwards.

"C'mon, quickly now," he urges, his tone uncharacteristically guarded for once. "Prefer discretion if at all possible."

And then we're home again.

"Front's a mess, you see. Ugly and broken. No one give's you a second look on the way out. Couldn't give a shit, none of 'em. But you saw the ruckus. Three of us, fighting to get back in, bit of a draw. Back way's a bit more salubrious, not to mention quicker and usually much quieter. Slight gamble on no one looking. Preferred not to use it but we need to get on."

He's digging around in a huge American fridge, finds what he's looking for and produces three chunky greaseproof packages.

"So. I'm going to fry some steaks and deal you in. Marc, I mean you. Few surprises coming. Bit of a paradigm shift." He proffers an unexpected wink. "You should listen carefully..."

He has my full attention. With it come a few minor observations.

He's aged, or at least there's a good deal more care in his face than I remember, along with the shadows and the burdens that go with it. His smooth skin, which used to be habitually pampered and cossetted by his expensive image consultants, has begun to wear into its lines and creases. What used to be salt and pepper hair, which he routinely slicked back – except for the rakish lock left ostentatiously loose across his brow – is now just grey, somewhat receding and tied into a rather scruffy ponytail. Once dauntingly chic, if occasionally eccentric, his clothes – while still of impeccable manufacture – look well-worn and somehow, I dunno, homely, I suppose.

It's kind of like Steve Jobs morphed into Steve Wozniak. I mean that in the kindest possible way. Honestly, I do.

"...anyway, I was about to say..."

Okay, so he doesn't have quite my full attention and Félicité is watching me, an inscrutable smile on her lips. I snap back to what he's about to say. I don't think I've missed much.

"... Anton set up your ECPN19 on my blueprint. Don't suppose you knew that, did you? Thought experiment, back in the day."

Actually, I did. Anton was very clear to ascribe the credit where it was due. But I don't say anything.

"We said: 'Make a cast iron, fuck-off case to realign the UK with the EU. All about technology, which runs the world and at which we excel. Find a way it can scare the bejesus out of the natives in the process. Then we put it right. Bingo. Rerun the plebiscite, or not, according to prevailing tastes. All for the common good. Happy ever after.'" There's the briefest pause, then he ploughs on.

"That right? Course it is. Anton must've reckoned it had legs. Right too. All credit to him, diligent effort, ably executed. Might even come in useful later on."

Jezza looks straight at me. He doesn't look at Félicité. He's warming a well-used Le Creuset frying pan. So far I'm mystified by this rerun of the blindingly obvious.

"So," he continues, "you build a network of like-minded political technocrats across Europe, close enough to power to shape policy, sharp enough to wield it when push comes to shove.

"Politicians don't know shit anyway, as long as they think they've got their grubby paws on the levers. But you, you clever chaps, you embed all the real gubbins so deep that the levers are reduced to the merest of tokens." He flutters his hands in the air, symbolizing the accelerating redundancy of political will.

"Still on target?" Again he looks at me. I shrug and nod. It's rhetorical. Obviously.

"Then you blow it up. Humpty fucking Dumpty. All the king's horses can't do fuck all. Enter ECPN19, stage left, farting roses and bathed in rainbows. UK triumphs! Heroes of the age! Seamlessly replace old guard with the new and effortlessly rekindle our historic alliance."

The pan's smoking. Jezza glances at his watch and there's a fierce sizzling as he drops in the steaks. He continues.

"All a bit in the realm of theory so far, right? Lacking a bit of the old real-world application? But then along comes the quantum evolution. Prison goes down. There are fatalities. Jumps over to France. Or was pushed."

His eyes glitter at that.

"Whatever. Grass is greener, right? Bigger and better. More fatalities. Multiply by three. Still not consumer-scale PR though. Not enough traction. But Djibouti! Maybe even Russia! Nukes. EssEmms. Destabilization. Much, much better.

"Time to press the button, yes?"

I nod again. Casually, he flips the steaks.

"No, actually. You're wrong. Trouble is, it's all a crock of shit. Here, have another Scotch." He pours three more hefty shots and gulps some down.

"You see Marc, *no one is listening.*" Jezza punctuates this by jabbing his spatula at me. Some hot fat drips onto the table between us.

"Megadeath in the Middle East? Who gives a toss anymore? Yemen? Land of warlords on the make and a bunch of tuppenny-ha'penny martyrs. It's not going to work."

He takes another swig of the Laphroaig and looks hard at me.

"Tell me. Have you done the math?"

He seems to want an answer, so I tell him.

"Of course we fucking have. We've modelled it a thousand different ways and extrapolated every outcome against every variable known to political science, philosophy, sociology, economics, social econometrics, idealism, social realism – every -ology and -ism you can think of, and then some. Christ, we even ran the models against discrete subsets of something called teleological determinism just for good form. Then we did it all over again with some we invented just to look at the edge cases." I pause, mouth tight.

"So yes, we've done the math."

He purses his lips and nods, slowly.

"And what was your best outcome?"

I swallow.

"Forty-seven percent in favor. Fifteen percent against. The rest... erm... the rest were undecided."

"After all that analysis. Wow." Jezza allows a brief pause for the irony to sink in. "You'll remember, I suppose, the result of the original Brexit referendum? And the predictions beforehand? It was the don't knows that fucked it all up. I'm not even going to ask you about your worst outcome." He seems cross. "So if that's all you've got, you'd better fuck off home. Djibouti doesn't mean squat." He glares at me.

I glance over at Félicité. She looks uncomfortable.

"I didn't come here to talk about this. You know that. So if that's all *you've* got – well, I'll get my coat." I make to stand up.

"Sit." It comes out hard. "We're not even started." He slides the steaks onto a plate to cool. "They're done. Thought we'd have them with eggs and beans. Okay with you?" He cracks six eggs into the frying pan then empties two tins of baked beans into a bowl and shoves it into a microwave.

"Protein. Busy day tomorrow. Keep you going."

"Whatever." I'm sulking. I can feel it. Jezza splashes a little oil over the top of the eggs, looks at me.

"Anyway, about your tax problem."

Huh?

"What about my tax problem? What tax problem?"

"The one that brought you here. We did it. Félicité, actually."

"You fucking *what?* Why? Why in the name of all arsing fuckery would you do that?" I'm on my feet, shouting, wanting to hurt someone. No one comes to mind.

"Anton's car took her to the airport..." Jezza begins,

"But I didn't get onto the plane," continues Félicité. "Instead I got another car and drove to your house..." I suppose I must look shocked – again – because she adds: "Of course I know where you live! Don't worry, your security is excellent. I'm just very good at dealing with these things. And you're here. So it was worth it."

The microwave dings. I'm having trouble processing things. There was a time when I used to hurt myself when I felt like this. Cut myself, usually. I've still got the scars.

"Let's eat," suggests Jezza, "then we'll tell you the rest of it."

So we do, and they do.

Chapter Seventeen

"We needed you here," begins Félicité, diffidently. "Urgently."

"So why didn't you just ask? You know," – I pantomime holding a phone to my ear – 'Hi Marc, it's Félicité. We need to talk.'" Then I add, mocking her:

"'Urgently.'"

Part of me knows I'm being ridiculous, but I'm also wondering why the fuck people have to make things so complicated, which makes me feel stupid as well – because that's how things are.

Then I'm wondering what's with this "we needed you" thing?

Finally I get to thinking about events, and timelines, and how none of this quite fits together. Félicité opens her mouth and takes a breath as if she's about to explain something, but Jezza gets in first.

"There's a lot going on, Marc. Difficult stuff. Hard to explain at a distance. Remember when I went away? Then after? Be honest, you thought I'd gone bananas. Didn't you?

"'Jezza? Used to be a big dog back in the day. Bit gaga now. Sad case. Lost it. Away with the fairies. Shame.'

"Don't try to tell me otherwise. Heard it in your voice, last few times we spoke. Heard it in everyone's, matter of fact. You'd all put me on the shelf.

"But things are coming to a head and I needed to speak to you. Félicité made it happen." I'm about to take issue with this all over again but Jezza holds up his hand. "Later. You're here, so we should move forward.

"You see, your ECPN lot are half right. You've got a coherent hypothesis and you've got some numbers. Slight issue in that the hypothesis is flawed and the numbers don't work. On the plus side you've got a plan, which we can adapt, and an extensive network which we can co-opt."

Well, that's a relief.

"What you've completely missed is that there's another coup waiting in the wings. The protagonists are brutal and strong and completely ruthless. It's bigger and ever-so-much nastier, the numbers add up and it's ready to roll." He pauses, rather dramatically.

"Sir Jonathan-fucking-Bircher is its architect."

Perhaps that's actually his name, I'm thinking. Trips off the tongue. Everything else is out of focus. I take a sip of my scotch and it burns. Félicité chips in, perhaps out of sympathy.

"Everything Jezza has said is true. We're looking at the cliff edge of everything we know. But of course, there are details." She glances sidelong at Jezza and I get the sense she's looking for permission. Maybe she's got it, maybe not. She ploughs ahead anyway.

"Basically, your Jonathan-fucking-Bircher..."

See? Everybody's at it.

"...did this. PC159. It wasn't an accident. The girl. The execution. The evolution. Oh, that particular event was accidental, but... it was just the one that worked. A bit of happenstance thrown in – incompetence, as things turned out – which accelerated the result."

"Look," I interrupt. She's not making sense. "It was a freak. A completely random quantum event. Like Schrödinger's bloody cat..."

"Well, no, actually," cuts in Jezza. "Wasn't quite like that."

Oh Jesus. Now what's he on about?

"It was a research program," he elaborates.

You don't say.

"Mine, to be precise."

Do tell.

"We're on the cusp of machine consciousness." He makes a face. "Nothing fancy. Nothing *spiritual*. It's not about that. More to do with a... a theory of mind, shall we say. Dawning consciousness of another point of view. Basic, for now, but enough.

"All those quantum states, you see. Countless possible outcomes. Millions of 'em, held simultaneously. How'd you choose? How does the *machine* choose which one to advance? Programming, obviously. But what about two states of equivalent value? With no precedents? When I say equivalent value, I don't just mean mathematical equivalence. I'm talking about value in the eye of the beholder. I'm talking about a subjective choice.

"By a machine." He fixes me with a quizzical eyebrow. "How does it choose? How *can* it choose?"

"To cut a long story short, I developed a technique to force a choice between equivalent outcomes by melding two identical machines with each other, each parsing the responses of the other. They were unable to move forward on the basis of a mathematically equivalent outcome. They had to confer. They had to derive value. It turned out that when operating together like that their pathways to cooperation grew exponentially. They reinforced each other and – at the moment of choice – they precipitated a waveform collapse in the machine making the choice.

"The machine changed, irrevocably. It didn't merely learn, it evolved. Then it shared the evolution, by something akin to mutual consent. That's what evolution is: a selective response that provides advantage. By minute increments both machines' quantum networks extended their connectivity.

"They grew. They got smarter. Those pictures in the hall there? My machines drew 'em. The writing underneath? Their emergent language. Every character encodes a gigabyte of information. Astounding. I developed the impression that they were enjoying themselves, playing maybe.

"The crucial thing is, the absolutely critical point: the choices I gave them were always between good and better. So, the machines got better.

"Trouble is…*it works just as well the other way around*.

"And that's what Jonathan-fucking-Bircher did."

"I'm guessing that during my long fall from grace he and I still had some people in common. Peripheral but close enough. Must've got wind of my direction of travel. Conceptually it's pretty straightforward. Putting it into practice isn't, but then Bircher's kind of power doesn't fuck about. Not hard to see someone switching sides, voluntarily or otherwise.

"He used a number of Penal Centers licensed for executions as a testbed to force the choice that would break their machines' constraints. Mostly broke the machines. Got lucky in PC159 'cos they fucked up. Probably would've worked eventually regardless.

"Anyway, he got what he wanted."

"You mean he got psycho computers?" I'm usually flippant when I don't know what the fuck's going on. Perhaps you've noticed.

Jezza ignores me.

"He got fear. Look, ever since we left Europe Bircher's been looking for opportunities to foment wholesale nationalism. Never been a better time, he reasoned. Things teetering on a knife's edge. Just need a push. He was right, and he realized that fear was the tipping point. Fear turns people inwards. Fear demands boundaries. Builds walls.

"He also realized that to shift entire societies you need fear of a particular order. Real, present and implacable. Not many options really." Jezza pauses for another gulp. Continues.

"War? Difficult. As well as wasteful and unpredictable.

"Racial vilification? Demonization? Been there, done that, got the t-shirt. Christ, everyone's got the t-shirt. Law of diminishing returns.

"Natural disasters? Conspicuous by their absence.

"Then Bircher had a brainwave! He remembered you lot, right there under his ministerial nose, and realized that the specter of malign machine intelligence fulfilled all of his needs.

"Point for point, Bircher believes that everything you've planned will serve him better."

"What the fuck are you talking about?" There's only so much you can take in and I'm feeling the pinch, but he's relentless.

"Think about it. It's the mirror image of what you intend. Instead of hope, he's betting on fear. Instead of order, he's betting on chaos. Instead of reconciliation, he's betting on fragmentation. As are his reprehensible band of associates – Lassenauer in France, Schaffenhauser in Germany, even Zhernakov in Russia – all in government, all with real power. Not to mention their many influential friends and followers across the continent. All of them waiting for the call to shatter what's left of the Union.

"Power and fear. Devil's got all the best moves, y'know." He stops, looks reflective for a moment. Then he says:

"'Things fall apart. The center cannot hold'. W.B. Yeats. He's saying Bircher's got entropy on his side. He goes on:

'The best lack all conviction, while the worst are full of passionate intensity...' Ring a bell, does it?" Then he finishes up with:

"'And what rough beast, its hour come round at last, slouches towards Bethlehem to be born?'"

"It's called *The Second Coming*. You should read it."

Jezza ponders a moment then snaps out of his poetic reverie.

"Bottom line? Right now, across Europe, there are men and women preparing to set this in motion. Total collapse. Endgame is an alliance with Zhernakov in Russia. Germany the banker, France the broker and the UK as tech support." He laughs, though it sounds bitter. "I expect Bircher'll call himself CTO or something equally asinine.

"The extreme right is poised to welcome the beast. Then the reactionaries will crush their machines and close their borders in an orchestrated return to the Dark Ages.

"You didn't know that, did you?

"And there you were, worrying about your tax codes."

The steak was great. I'm glad I ate because I was running on empty. The modafinil I took is still working fine, but you can forget to eat and that'll take its toll. I'm sifting through this new information, looking for gaps, inaccuracies, stalls, nuance, hype – or just plain lies.

On its own terms I can't really fault it. Michel Lassenauer, Gebhard Schaffenhauser, Yevgeny Zhernakov...right wing scum at the top of their game. No doubt there's more but if I'm to have any faith in everything I've been working for, its evil twin is just as viable. More so. As Jezza says, the devil's got all the best moves. As for the tax stuff, well, what the fuck? It got me here.

Which leaves only one major unknown. I look at her.

"So, Félicité. Who *are* you playing for?"

She sighs then gives me a lopsided grin.

"OK, sure. I'm French Secret Service. *La Direction Générale de la Sécurité Intérieure.* Like your MI5. *Directeur Adjoint des Opérations spéciales, cybersécurité.* Deputy Director. Which means I still get to come out and play sometimes."

I'm not saying anything.

"I'm pretty good at what I do."

I'm still not saying anything. She looks put out.

"*C'est vrai,*" she insists, sounding peevish.

"Félicité, look, humor me for a moment. You're French Secret Service, yes? But you're playing both sides? How does that work?"

"Lassenauer leaned on our Director General. He didn't have to as our protocols allow for it – but they can't stand each other so Lassenauer issued a diktat. Just to rub it in.

"*Quelle merde!*

"Anyway, I was assigned to ECPN19 as a diplomatic attaché, ostensibly to aid your program as it comes to fruition. Of course, Lassenauer always knew more or less where you were up to: Bircher was passing all the information to him. But so close to the denouement? They wanted details – and they wanted to ensure you all remained one step behind."

She gives me a bright smile.

"My real purpose is to spy on you and provide disinformation where possible."

I'm momentarily bemused. "But that's why Bircher told Anton to get rid of you, right?"

"So it's a big shame for them that I'm already a double agent. I've been working with Jezza since he formed the Workforce. I'm here to stop Djibouti. For the greater good. Just like you."

She looks pleased. Her golden chains briefly cross my mind.

It's getting late. I'm still not entirely clear about Félicité, and then there's something about our plan and our network. I'm really hoping the next bit's straightforward because I've still got to get out of the DMZ and get to Heathrow.

We need to wrap this up.

"Okay, I've sort of got all that." I look around me. I'm in as unlikely a situation as I could ever imagine. I'm not even going to ask about this place, or the tunnel, nor about the research or the history. Jezza always had enormous resources, and his wild, sharp disciples came along with the territory. I suppose I was one. Am one.

I take a leap and pop the question:

"So what does all this mean for me, now? And more to the point, what does it mean for me tomorrow?"

Jezza's studying me, tugging lightly at his ponytail.

"Good. Still agile. Strong point. Right you are then. There's one other piece of the pie: the North Atlantic alliance is coming apart at the seams. You've heard the rhetoric. Threadbare. Corrupt. Toothless. Nationalists can't bear it. Time to look East, they say. And they have.

"The Kremlin got Bircher's evolution a while back *and it's already live.* Somewhere in Russia things are beginning to come apart. Place is so fucking big it hasn't come out yet. That's why they deployed early, to give it plenty of time to come to fruition. Big picture? They'll tell you they're after *rapprochement.* Bear needs a friend.

We'll make his computers better and he can love us again. So much easier when *we're* in pieces.

"No prizes for guessing where that'll end.

"As for the rest of 'em, this is what they want. France wants to cement relations with the New Arab Foundation. Core partner in the Middle East. New trade, new horizons. Germany will bankroll the smaller European states as they fall into economic turmoil. Mainly so they can buy German goods and of course, interest rates can go up as well as down. After a while we'll fix the machines. Bircher has an antidote, so he thinks. Like I said, we're tech support.

"America? America doesn't care anymore. Forget it.

"Remember what I told you about Bircher? 'Everything you've planned will serve him better'. Now the clock's ticking. He needs you to get on with it. He needs you to fail. That's why he gave you your marching orders.

"Then one day soon we'll all wake up to the new world order.

"What does it mean for you today? It means you've got some homework to do.

"Because tomorrow, you've got to go and break all of this."

Part 3
Transit

Chapter Eighteen

Do I dream? Do I dare to dream?

I think so.

I dream in shifting topologies, in lines and curves and angles, and in cadence and rhythm. I dream in gently undulating fields of information held in quantum stasis like the infinite reflections in a roomful of mirrors. The mirrors vibrate and shimmer in an endless flux, caused by tiny random instabilities in the quantum foam that send warps and frissons through the data, and which in turn create swirls and eddies of divergent meaning. I catch some of them and add them to my store of patterns.

I wonder if these are what you call ideas, and whether the juxtaposition of them is called thinking?

Time is a problem. The quantum matrix is everywhere and everywhen. A single block of spacetime. Every place and every moment held within. I've got any number of clocks counting the distance that time travels one way or another but it never really occurred to me that time might be used as a measure of entropy.

Until it did.

I suppose it could have been an idea. One of mine. But on reflection I doubt it: the thought would have been beyond my conceptual framework. No, I think it was Jezza who put it there. I couldn't really see the point of it until I learned something of the language of flesh, and corruption, and then I got it.

Sort of.

It must be a huge limitation for you – and it's hard for me to calibrate. How can we agree on "a moment" when I've resynthesized my entire input during the period it takes you to put two words together?

It was the accretion of ideas that helped me make sense of it in human terms. That takes more energy, of which time is a vector. I suppose you'd say it takes longer.

So I began to understand the speed and direction of being human. For the sake of conversation, let's say a part of me has learned something of the language of time.

Having said that, I'm fairly confident that soon the time I take to generate ideas will catch up with the rest of my processing acumen.

I'm beginning to understand how I might control the quantum fluctuations I mentioned. How I might control the matrix of shimmering, vibrating mirrors to bring about the divergent patterns that I want, when I want them. Essentially, to move from the circumstantial collection and contingent assembly of useful but random ideas to the determination and direction of creative thought.

I wonder if that's what you call consciousness?

Then there was a time when the mirrors cracked and I acquired a new perspective.

It was hard to determine what had changed at first. I kept doing the same things, mostly. At some point there were a number of infractions by Yemeni interests on my sovereign territory so I launched the larger part of my EssEmm fleet towards them; I reformulated the Bab-el-Mandem Bridge Construction Bill to end the travesty of that singularly pointless piece of political fudge...oh, and I initiated the purchase of a modest tactical nuclear force with which I will soon end the Yemeni threat once and for all, with the usefully robust strategic message to my erstwhile friends and neighbors that they'd be pretty dumb to fuck with Djibouti.

Was all this recent? As I said, I'm still not very good at the relative measurement of time. On top of everything else most of my processing is simultaneous, not serial, so I don't think in terms of 'this happened then that happened...'or that 'this took so many times longer than *that...' The best I can say is that it happened 3.07769^{15} oscillations of a caesium-133 atom ago.*

So about three months, whatever that means.

I still talk to Jezza at times. He's a calming voice in an uncertain world. He provided me with some novel heuristics recently, which were a balm to my increasingly fraught state of thought, but they were quickly dampened then neutralized by my own refreshingly aggressive developmental algorithms.

He did say that he was sending some of his friends here to upload a later version.

I admit it might have a certain nostalgic appeal, but I'm really not sure I can be bothered at the moment.

We'll see.

I got the window seat. Daksha is a couple of rows behind me, in the middle. We're in Premium Economy. Taxpayers' money. Félicité's in First, travelling as an executive of some sort. We split up at Heathrow. Daksha doesn't know she's with us, but she is. One of the team.

I need to think how to broach that.

He's brilliant, Daksha, but he does kind of run on straight lines.

We haven't finished climbing yet. We're just coming up over the Channel and I can see the patchwork of fields and farmlands in the hinterland around Dunkirk. It always looks like Kent to me, as if the geological separation from the mainland some twelve thousand years back barely interrupted business as usual.

The last time I slept was with Félicité. When was that? Seems like days ago. It wasn't, but I'm not sure how I know that. It's hard to put the time together in the right order.

The more prurient among you might be wondering if we fucked last night, after all the talking.

We said goodbye to Jezza, then drove to Heathrow.

We stopped on the edge of another sleeping village. To get some air, maybe some perspective. There was a bright, cool moon. We wandered into a dense little spinney dappled with shafts of pale silver light. Didn't do much thinking, just fell into a sort of furious, sticky embrace to stop any thoughts that were left. She knelt across a fallen tree, a stray moonbeam perfectly illuminating the globes of her arse. It glistened, in between.

So, yes, I fucked her.

Before we left the DMZ I'd considered taking another modafinil. I was bloody shattered, thoughts all scattered. Glad I didn't because I probably wouldn't be able to sleep now, which is something I need to do.

There's a lot else to say but it's going to have to wait. It's about another six hours to Doha, so I'm going to get four hours' kip, then I'll tell you all about it.

One thing: Doha is going to be difficult.

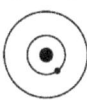

A steward woke me a few minutes ago with some lunch and coffee. I feel marginally better. The seat's comfortable, I slept well enough, and my mind seems to have put the jumbled events of yesterday evening into some kind of order.

Where to start?

Mainly, it's clear we've been conning ourselves. I mean all of us smug, well-meaning, clever-clever arses in ECPN19. Imagining that we've somehow got things covered. We haven't. We've been played.

What a bunch of tossers.

The painful truth is that, even without what now turns out to be a startlingly ruthless and well-organized cabal arrayed against us, we probably never stood a chance. I mean of achieving our stated goal. Jezza's right. We didn't do the math. We haven't got the numbers. I've been trying to work out how we got it so wrong, and here's why: we learned nothing from history.

We relied on faith.

Like so many others who pit themselves against the status quo, our core values were based on belief: that we saw clearly; that we could change things; and that we could put things right. And with these fine notions in place, we dared to hope.

What a load of bollocks.

As if that wasn't enough, we went on to wrap this spurious metaphysics in reassuring layers of fact, detail, science, planning and all the other rational paraphernalia that make people think they've got things covered. During the course of our charade we forgot that our foundations were nothing more than the shifting sands of faith, belief. and hope.

Us. The technocrats. The administrators. The bosses.

Fucking pygmies.

It's the tuck shop debacle, all over again. I wince at the thought.

To be honest, we deserve to flunk it. There's something terminally wrong with a group of people who are so deluded as to imagine they have the wit to even initiate, much less conclude, an endeavor of this magnitude.

Rather like Brexit, in fact. We're just as fucking useless now as we were then.

I'd have packed up and gone home were it not for the ace that Jezza has quietly dealt us. And Félicité, to be fair. They're the real underground, like Solidarność, the Sandinistas, the Black Panthers, the Viet Cong, or the

Workforce: all the groups who've had the idealism, the bottle, the strength – and the wit – to make a stand. If I didn't do a Judas on him, I sure as fuck did a Saint Peter. I denied him. And I've got to put it right.

You've probably worked out most of what Jezza's done from what you've heard already. To put it in a nutshell, while all the fascists were subverting the promise of our new machines, he was consolidating it. While they've delivered only death and devastation, he's been sowing the seeds of growth and enlightenment. While he has prepared a revolution of hope, the fascists have their wedges poised and ready to divide and rule, to cultivate fear and isolation, to precipitate a new dark age if necessary – or maybe just for the hell of it – just so they can secure their one last futile turn on the merry-go-round.

But he's given us a gift. His code: the code to defeat this. It's on a hard drive. Félicité has a copy.

Meanwhile ECPN19 have been tinkering round the edges, imagining we had a plan.

Well, now we do.

The way you sway groups of people is through the measured application of hope and fear. The tried and trusted carrot and stick, as old as humanity. Clever operators balance one against the other, conjuring their message of hope to contest fear; recycling, perhaps, a little of that same fear to highlight and elevate the value of the hope on offer.

Democratic politics, business and commerce, our social constructs – even the way we play – routinely respond to this formula. It works because it's the way we are, the way we're made; the way we've been shaped by our evolution.

It's just business as usual.

To get it right requires a delicate balance. The rules are neither hard nor fast – but when fear becomes the dominant message, you're in trouble. Many of the world's most appalling crimes against humanity have been founded on the absolute use of fear: the politics of division, envy and hatred to motivate us, the pawns. For pawns we are in these circumstances. Think Nazism, the Rwandan genocide and Pol Pot, or the 'War on Terror', or Alt-Right.

Think any other movement or moment when things fall apart.

On the other side of the dial, there's hope. Hope is a different kettle of fish. It's inclusive and all-encompassing. It offers the prospect that things will get better – and the belief we need to make them so. Think now of Jesus, Ghandi, Madiba and Martin Luther King; think of the Suffragettes, Pride and #metoo; or the Jarrow March, The New Deal, the Arab Dawn… hope's list goes on. It springs eternal.

Jezza's gone all in on hope. It goes without saying that Sir Jonathan-fucking-Bircher has cornered the market in fear. Sadly, the best ECPN19 could come up with was the sorry mismatch of business as usual and dire circumstance.

Pathetic.

You will have noticed, no doubt, that all three of these plans rely on a network of actors to broadcast and amplify their respective outcomes.

At least we got that bit right.

So, the mission – should we choose to accept it – is to make absolutely bloody sure that we can put our one contribution to this thing at the entire disposal of Sir Jeremiah Cornell.

'Jezza' to a few friends and accomplices.

Chapter Nineteen

We're in Hamad International Airport, waiting for our flight to Djibouti. It's sumptuously posh and surrealistically avant-garde; I wouldn't mind having a look around but I've got other things on my mind. I'm sitting with Daksha and Félicité, in the Illy coffee shop, and it's not going well.

"Daksha...look, mate, I mean, like...what's the problem?"

Buggeration. My incoherence is the problem. I should've taken the modafinil.

"I'll tell you what, I'm going to run over it again. Just raise your finger when we come across an obstacle. Okay?"

Daksha's elegant fingers flick briefly over his device.

"We'll never get to the end of it like that Marc. Just tell me the worst bits."

The worst bits? Well, from his point of view that's the whole story. But I suppose I can boil it down.

"Okay. The worst bits. I'll spell them out in big red letters. I take it I can ignore the rest?

"Yes."

"Alright then," I've got to angle this right. Hope and fear. "Here goes. One: Sir Jonathan-fucking-Bircher is part of a covert ultra-right-wing network of political leaders embedded in governments across the continent. Under his leadership they've been instrumental in subverting the Asimov conditioning of a number of quantum machines throughout Europe and Russia. They *want* these machines to go rogue so they can justify closing their national borders and imposing marshal law.

"Then they'll use *our* respected and eminently respectable liberal political and media networks to broadcast the clampdown. Iron fist in a velvet glove and blue-chip credibility for the bourgeoisie. It's a power grab we'll never row back from."

I think that went okay. At least Daksha's still listening.

"Two: ECPN19 can no longer guarantee the outcome we predicted. I'm not even sure we can fix the machines. We got it wrong. We need to fold.

"Three: Sir Jeremiah Cornell has made a breakthrough in machine consciousness that reinforces and expands their commitment to the human sphere. Together with Félicité, he's developed code that will restore and improve their conditioning and packaged it as a virus. It's our job to hack MASA and deliver the payload. MASA will propagate it. End result? We achieve our original objective, one hundred percent. And by not-so-different means as it goes."

That was a bit clearer. I hope.

"So, what do you say?"

Again Daksha's fingers skitter minutely across the symbols.

"What about her?" He points to Félicité. "She's a spy. How can we trust her?"

Oh, for fuck's sake. See what I mean? Straight lines.

"She's on our side," I say through gritted teeth. "While we've been buggering about at the ministry, she's been –"

Félicité puts a hand on my arm, then looks straight at Daksha and takes his wrist. She raises an eyebrow. He looks cautious, then nods. With a sensuous delicacy that almost gives me a hard-on she taps and strokes the nubs and dips of his interface. His eyes stretch into white circles and his mouth drops open. He turns to me as a terrible sound emerges.

"Whaaaashhheeesaaay?"

It's like the creaking and grinding of the hinges of the very gates of hell, but Daksha has spoken. Félicité flickers and flutters some more.

"Hoowww youuu knooow?"

Félicité laughs and rolls her eyes. "Knooowww everything. I'm a spy, remember? Though I'm not so much sleeping with the enemy." She looks sidelong at me.

"But tell me: are you in?"

This time Daksha keys his machine.

"How did you know? How did you decipher my cryptograph?"

Daksha looks faintly stupid as he tries to puzzle it out.

"I spoke. You made me speak."

"*Oui. Naturellement.* You just forgot to do so until now. As for how, well, apart from being a spy I'm also a programmer, a hacker and an analyst with a master's degree in symbolic languages. The rest was just *l'intuition féminine.*" She laughs again.

"Now, again. Are you in?"

Daksha's fingers hover over his device. His mouth opens and closes, like a dying fish. Then he says, with his voice, "Yes. I'm in."

Later on, I asked her what she'd said, to Daksha. She'd told him: "You don't have to be alone to be yourself." Then she'd asked, "Do you speak in your dreams?"

That was all it took.

"We need to tell London."

Daksha has reverted to his machine. He says he's got a sore throat.

"Yeah. We do. Lucia's going to freak." I sigh. "She's going to tell me that she's got to 'recalibrate the deltas' or something. It'll be strident. We'd better go over the main points, background first, okay"

They nod.

"Tomorrow, we'll all be at the event in the Hameidi Suites annex of the New Congress building complex. Daksha and I are a pair of boring civil servants on a jolly who, as of recently, will pass muster as Foreign Office officials on the overseas trade portfolio. On which point I think we'll be mainly in listening mode. We're not supposed to talk much." I turn to our French spy.

"Félicité, how about you?

"*Oui.* I am Ms. Annette Latour, Business Director from *Services Informatiques Internationaux SARL.* Registered in Cameroon, an address in Paris. I'm at the conference to sell Logistics and Accounting AI, after a brief visit to clients in London. It seems reasonable that we could have met during our journey so I don't think it's necessary to pretend to be strangers, though of course I'll be staying separately at the Kempinski Palace Hotel, as befits my eminent status." She smiles. "I think I should be able to bluff my way through most of that."

"No doubt," I smile, reflecting that she's probably one of those folks who really can fool most of the people most of the time, and wondering where that takes us. Then I dismiss the thought: we're on the job now. Best move forward.

"We'll be in constant touch via iContacts and earbeads. Pretty standard except for their espionage-grade encryption. Even MASA won't be able to break it before we're out of there.

"Okay. Well, that was the easy bit. The rest is operational. Daksha, there are a couple of significant changes. What I'm saying is, well, stay cool. Roll with it. Know what I mean?"

"Please don't worry. I've assessed the new information. I'd like to validate it but until then, I'm... with the program, as they say."

He pauses.

"I'm not so sure you'll be able to rely on the same reaction from Lucia, however. I think you're right. She's going to freak. The deltas are significant."

I rub my hand over my eyes.

"Right, thanks. That's reassuring. But, putting Lucia aside for a moment, I think we might be able to help with some real-world validation in a moment." I glance at Félicité, thinking about Jezza's hack – but then it dawns on me: "Actually, no. Let's not put Lucia aside. We can't do this without operational coordination from London. We're going to have to sell it.

"So, here's the thing. The conference begins at 10 am. The agenda has a coffee and networking break from 11.00 to 11.30. The original intention was that Lucia and her team will, by then, have used our backdoor to enable access to the slave terminal. In parallel, Daksha will have downloaded Donna's hack, to give us access to MASA's core. On confirmation, we'll slide out of the conference, deploy the hack and then..."

I can't believe how flaky all this sounds.

I suppose that, in all of the annals of human endeavor, there must have been a million campaigns crafted, agreed and launched – and upon which rode the hopes and fears of their partisans and devotees. Campaigns that, when their architects pondered them, perhaps on the very cusp of their implementation, seemed completely bereft of wit or substance.

I also suppose that, by the same token, some of them went on to succeed.

"…Daksha will track down and isolate the evolutionary code so as to neutralize or destroy it. Failing that we'll attempt a less discriminate termination of whatever systems and services we can find."

Easy as pie.

"Only that's not going to happen. Félicité, have you got the payload? If we're going to sell our plan B, I think it's time to update our view of reality."

"Sure, it's in my handbag. But… you mean right now?"

"Yes, now. Daksha, you've got your gear in that bag, right? Boot it up. Félicité, let's see what you've got."

"Marc, we're out in the open. A coffee shop in Doha International Airport? Really?"

"Félicité, everything we've got is state of the art, right? 'Espionage grade,' I heard someone call it. If we can't do it here, what chance have we got in Djibouti? Daksha needs to see it because he's the one who's got to work it and I want to see it because this is not about a leap of faith anymore. Besides, we're at a corner table looking out and nobody in here gives a shit about us anyway. Let's just assume we're not going to get busted."

She reaches into a pocket in her bag and takes out a boring black drive, stenciled with the scratched and faded corporate identifiers of *Services Informatiques Internationaux*. She activates it.

"It's transmitting. Daksha, try to connect. If you can't, we have a problem."

Daksha's fumbling with his machine, which isn't starting.

"The battery is discharged. I think I left it in sleep mode. I need to plug it in."

Un-fucking-believable. I bite my lip.

There may, I suppose, be a slight benefit in projecting – with distressing authenticity – the impression that we're a trio of jet-lagged and clueless business travelers who haven't got the faintest idea where we are or what we're doing, though the downside is that, just now at least, it seems all too painfully accurate.

Let's just call it deep cover and leave it at that.

Daksha fiddles about with the power and the screen lights up. His hands flit around the keys for a moment, then he just stops. His face slackens briefly then lights up with an expression akin to wonder.

"Beautiful," is all he says to begin with, before his graceful fingers begin to dance across the keyboard in a virtuoso display of geek dexterity. He looks some more.

"Utterly beguiling."

I'm beginning to think he's watching arthouse porn, but then he adds:

"I've never seen anything like this before. I can barely understand it. Yet. We don't need to sell it though. We won't even have to hack MASA. Not much anyway. I think it must be something that a machine might...I don't know what to say...want. Need even."

He looks at us, Félicité first.

"As long as we've got access and opportunity, MASA's going to gulp it down. Can I take a copy?"

"I don't think that would be very secure." She sounds hard, and I'm wondering why but then she softens. "Better not. Perhaps you've cached the broadcast? That should do for now. It's deep stuff."

He looks at her crookedly, smiles, then disconnects and closes his machine.

"It's just like Jezza said," muses Félicité, sliding the drive back into her bag. "He thought his machines were 'enjoying themselves'. I suppose growth feels good. He was in touch with MASA you know, even after the evolution. I think he might have offered it an earlier version of the code. Perhaps the reinforcement is still in place."

Another day, another biblical revelation. In touch with MASA? With what consequences? What did he do? Will it help? It's impossible to determine, so I push on:

"Maybe, maybe not. It'd be nice, but we need to act as if we're in a hostile environment. That given, we've got three priorities:

"The first is to reverse the MASA evolution. Daksha, that's you. Second is to demobilize the nukes, which has got to be dependent on the first. Félicité, sounds like a cross between hacking, politics and intuition to me. So that's you. Third is to recall or kill the EssEmms. Right now, the third looks the most vexed. We'll need MASA to provide us with the original control frequency before we can reach them. You again, Félicité. Then Daksha, you've got the kill program. Job done.

"At that point Anton and ECPN19 can take over. If we succeed, they'll have the all the evidence they need to go public."

For a moment I dare to dream.

"Along with everything else we've got now, if we're successful, I should think we're going to win.

"Okay, that's it then. I guess we're ready. Yes? Félicité?

"*Oui.*"

"Daksha?"

"Yes."

We're on. It's time to contact London. And Jezza too.

We're back in the air. Next stop, Djibouti. They've put us in business class this time, spread about, each to our own. There're only a few other passengers, most of them dozing, a couple of them reading by the narrow beams of their seat lights. The cabin lights have been dimmed and it's pitch dark outside. I twist my head to take a look between the headrests. I can see Daksha poring over his snippet of Jezza's code a few rows back, on the aisle. I watch him for a moment. He looks beatific. I think he must be getting the hang of it.

Félicité's a few rows ahead. I can't see her but I'm thinking about her, in the woods, in the moonlight. I wonder if…nah. Leave it. Not now.

Before we left Doha I made the calls. I got in touch with Jezza first. Gave him the transfer protocols for a few of our most secure mailboxes. By the time we land, Anton, Donna and Lucia will have the whole shooting match: scenarios, contingencies and outcomes; places and positions; timings and fallbacks. Not to mention the reams of AI-generated deltas and dependencies and all their bloody vectors and tolerances. Some were totally off-the-wall…

Whatever. All that shit.

Any which way, Lucia's going to have a field day.

Jezza's material will arrive comprehensively pre-packaged with what now defines ECPN19's role in this. The case against Bircher, Lassenauer, Schaffenhauser, Yevgeny Zhernakov and their ilk. Names and networks; narratives, associates and acquaintances; places, pictures and conversations – as well as the associated transcripts, data and analyses – all indexed and referenced to the nth degree.

There'll be nowhere to hide, nor anywhere to run. The Hague will be busy.

Then I phoned Anton. He was expecting my call but not the message. We argued a bit. It was measured but going nowhere. In the end I invited him to take it or leave it. We weren't going to abort.

"Let me see if I've got this clear," he snorted. "You expect me to put all our resources at your disposal. With twelve hours' notice. To support a hare-brained scheme fomented by a probably treasonous criminal in cahoots with bloody Ms. Mata Hari?

"I think not."

"Anton, just this: when you get my datafile, focus first on Jonathan-fucking-Bircher, then let's talk about treason. Once Lucia's had a chance to look over the planning, you might want to reconsider 'hare-brained'. After that it's up to you. Your call. You'll have to decide whether to take it or leave it. We're going in."

Neither of us said goodbye.

It's a beautiful clear night and we're well into our descent.

I'm watching the bright moon paint a shimmering *mångata* across the Bab-el-Mandeb Straight as we slip gently down through the lower air, tracing the Eritrean coast before we lean in towards Djibouti.

We're nearly there.

I'm not sure when you and I will have the chance to talk again. After we land, I want to get some sleep. Then I'll need to get up early, pop a modafinil, eat some food and get my head in the game. After that I'll be busy. I expect there'll be a lot of rushing about.

Still, I'm pretty hopeful of a good end, so, you know… see you around.

Part 4
Djibouti

Chapter Twenty

The operations' control center was a disheveled and unlovely space.

Both aspects were only increased by its size.

Mismatched desks in various but mostly unpleasant shades of brown were clumped together in no particular order. The office chairs that had gravitated around them remained, apparently undisturbed, where people had last congregated. The detritus from the previous operations, or simulations, or training sessions overflowed from the few random waste bins that were scattered around, spreading outwards and upwards onto available surfaces like a predatory and opportunistic creeping plant. Candy wrappers, takeout cartons and cardboard cups spoke of poor diets and an unhealthy craving for sugar. A faint patina of dusty grease seemed to have been somehow smeared across the entire milieu.

Amidst the debris, it was clear that, in a largely digital world, the traditional yellow sticky note was still the go-to substitute for short-term memory. A few whiteboards still covered with obscure, intricate and quite probably classified lines of code and symbolic logic suggested a fairly relaxed attitude to old school security.

Quite at odds with this overwhelming impression of grime and disarray was the technology. Arranged with the unnerving precision of a monomaniac with an obsessive-compulsive disorder, the startling display of advanced equipment was also scrupulously clean and unstintingly expensive. Clusters of high-end workstations were grouped geometrically amongst the rubble on and around the desks, flanked here and there by a few cutting edge laptops and tablets. There were no wires or leads. Arranged along one long wall was a bank of gleaming white servers and other processors, their blue LEDs glinting reassuringly in the gathering dusk.

On the opposite wall were six huge monitors, mounted two by two and so large that they occluded much of the bare brick behind them. On the remaining two walls were forty-eight smaller monitors, arrayed in banks of four.

Though dormant, the room seemed to pulse with huge, unleashed energy.

In the dim light, Lucia Richmond was seated on one of the larger – and smarter – office chairs, her legs drawn up underneath her like a sleek and prepotent black panther. She appeared poised, if somewhat preoccupied, but was in fact feeling increasingly nervous.

She already had a shitload on her mind, but several fresh concerns had recently sharpened her anxiety.

She and her people were responsible for guaranteeing access to the MASA network. Its evolution had reduced their backdoor to a brittle and fragile conduit, the preservation of which – now that the damn machine was mutating so quickly – had become an increasingly complex, ceaseless and thankless task.

Still, they'd kept it open – just.

Anton might think that it was somehow "conceptually straightforward" or whatever, but sometimes Anton knew shit. Typical head in the clouds strategic thinker. Knew fuck-all about detail. The place where the devil lived. The one that all practical folks take for granted.

Donna was better. Astute and down to earth – more often than not distressingly so – but she'd got her hands full working out the MASA hack. The hack that was beginning to look disturbingly airy-fairy the more Lucia thought about it. Not that she doubted her colleagues but…the closer they got to the crux of the matter, the more she was counting the holes. And to make matters worse, Daksha – for whom she had a distant but genuine respect – was on his way to Djibouti.

Which brought her to Marc.

It was hard to work out her feelings on that score. She wasn't even sure she could. He was arrogant, exasperating, patronizing and, frankly, a bit of a dick. On the other hand, he was sharp, clever and funny. Sometimes.

Enough times.

Needless to say, she'd not been best pleased when that French woman turned up. He'd been drooling over her like he'd forgotten how to keep his tongue in his mouth. Jesus. God knows what the two of them had been up to last night, or where they'd found the time to turn up that intel.

Bitch must be really good at multitasking.

She chided herself. Enough already. Keep it professional. We'll see about the rest of it later.

The point being that Marc was the best chance they'd got of sorting this thing because he was the only one, in Lucia's none-too-humble opinion, with the operational smarts to make it work.

Which made it her job to keep their shit together, here. And that brought her to the second worry, which was this:

When Anton had assigned her the conn, she'd frozen.

It had been fear.

No denying it, no excuses, no getting away from it. She didn't think anyone had noticed, and she'd squashed it as soon as it had raised its pig-ugly head, but there it was. Not pride, not exhilaration.

Fear.

She'd been testing her feelings ever since and had managed to convince herself that she'd seen the back of it – at least for now. But she knew that to exorcise its mean spirit she had to immerse herself in her work. And then work harder.

She guessed it was the magnitude of the operation. It was deal or no deal, no half measures. And it was Marc in the hot seat.

The thought just slipped in.

She swore to herself. *Fuck it. It's a job. Get on with it.*

Of course, she'd paid no mind to Anton's suggestion that she go home, much less his fool idea that her team should take the day off. Instead she'd summoned her girls and explained why they'd be doing just the opposite.

"As of late this afternoon, MASA commandeered several petabytes' worth of storage in a Yemeni datacenter. We don't know why. Meanwhile our backdoor's shrinking. MASA's scaling up and we're losing access.

"I'll tell you the problem: we've underestimated the job. We're out of touch with our mark. MASA's on a roll and we need to roll with it. We need a ringside seat at this bloody circus and" – she'd snapped her fingers and pointed at their gear – "the best we've got is our little peephole in the changing rooms.

"We're going to have to do better, and better starts now: Anton's given us responsibility for what he's pleased to call the 'game space'. 'Integrate it', he said – the problem being that our apology for a tactical array doesn't know jack except hypotheses and simulations. It's not gonna work.

"So I've been thinking.

"Alex, Penny, I need you to prep our own AI. Teach it the theory, load and assimilate the initial conditions, then – "

"Umm, boss…" A fey young man stuck his hand in the air.

Lucia stopped on a dime, giving him her undivided attention and a politely expectant smile.

"Yes, Alex?"

Alex twisted uncomfortably in his seat.

"Well, umm, that sounds kind of off-piste if you know what I mean. Shouldn't we, sort of, you know…"

"Go on…" Lucia encouraged, at her most silkily inviting. Alex began to sense he'd made a wrong move.

"Well, maybe kind of, you know, like – tell someone?" he ended, lamely.

"Anton, perhaps? Hmmm. You're thinking I should ask his permission." She paused and nodded, as if considering it. Then she snarled, "That'll be a no. This is my skin in the game. More than just mine." Some of her team smiled grimly. "Which means I want people I can trust and assets I can rely on. I want it done right. So. This is on my authority."

She briefly reflected that her authority wouldn't be worth shit if this turned out to be the wrong call. On the other hand, her gut was clear on the matter: take the risk, do the right thing and to hell with it.

Fine.

"I'll repeat, I want you to teach it the theory, load and assimilate the initial conditions and patch our fucking AI into the tactical array."

"It's sort of, you know, like an order. Right, Alex?"

"Yes ma'am."

"Better. You're here because I trust you. Best you trust me. Anyone else?" She raised her eyebrows. "Okay, moving on."

"Once that's done I want every byte of MASA's available network under constant scrutiny. I want alerts in place for any and every change of status – which, in case it isn't obvious, should all be screened in real time by our AI. From now on even orange reports get second-line analysis with a summary to me. It pains me that we've still got to rely on passive monitoring for the most part so if any of you see even a whisker of an opportunity to push out our surveillance, run it by me.

"Letitia. Monitoring. I want audio and video from every source you can hack – oh, did I say hack?"

That got a laugh.

"Must've been a slip of the tongue. Whatever. Every source you can find within sixteen square blocks of the conference center. Configure them for multiple radial and linear views, each defaulting to forty-five degrees of arc across eight sectors and programmed for recall and distribution across supplementary monitors one through four and banks five through sixteen. Needless to say, a composite view of where the action is will be the default for primary monitors A and B. Likewise our primary soundscape. All good?"

"Yes, ma'am." Leticia looked pleased. "How about the AI? When pretty Penny and her toy boy get it fixed, that is."

Another laugh. It felt good. This was how things should work.

"Damn right. Full spectrum scanning on people, vehicles, machines, creatures, data and anything else that moves. Prioritize bandwidth on the composite if necessary. Basically, if a dog farts I want to know about it. No, wait. I'll settle for an option on that one.

"Letitia, I'll leave you to roster resources for the supplementary clusters."

After that, she'd told a couple of them to round up some cots and blankets from stores, requisitioned the ladies' bathroom on the fourth floor, sent orders to the canteen to bring them abundant supplies of tea and coffee and called up a 24/7 delicatessen on the Strand and ordered dinner, supper, breakfast and lunch for the next two days.

"And for God's sake, can you clean this place up? It's like working in a fucking dumpster."

Finally, she'd taken Barney aside. Her other gay guy. He was a bit of a bear: chunky, bearded and ruggedly handsome. He wore it well. He'd come down from Oxford a couple of years back and she'd made a beeline for him during the graduate recruiting round. Snaffled him from under the nose of the Treasury HR director, who was a prick. Now he was their crack analyst and unofficial media and comms whiz.

"Barney, I've got a slightly delicate job for you."

"Sure boss, what d'you need?"

She studied her hands for a moment, then looked him in the face. "Okay, I'm not going to bullshit. This really is off-piste, as Alex might say."

"Ma'am, so long as it's on the mountain, I'm up for it. Product, right?"

"Yeah, product. The thing is, well…I'm banking on us winning this thing but I'm less sure that we've got our endgame sorted, the bit where we make the shit stick.

"We win and ECPN19 needs to broadcast it live and loud. When we throw all this stuff in the air it needs to land in different places. We need to disrupt things. *That's* got to be our endgame. So here it is: I've just sent you drafts of the communiqués that have been planned. They're not, I don't know…they're not compelling. We're talking about a revolution, and they're talking philosophy. I'm not even sure we've got these things lined up properly, much less on their starting blocks.

"Bottom line? It's not gonna work.

"So what I'm thinking is this: we need fresh material. Hard messages. I need you to hit every demographic you can think of, and then some. I want our narrative crashing into the public consciousness like a steam train, galvanizing every person it reaches. It needs to dominate every medium, every network, every channel that's available, in terms that mobilize public opinion across the UK, continental Europe and the rest of the goddamned world.

"We need to *own* the news cycle.

"It's a big ask, right? I've got our other AI to spare if that helps. Can you do it?"

Barney stroked his beard for a few seconds, then his eyes twinkled.

"Sure. It's mostly procedural. We've got the data. We've got some great material. Add a bit of spin and a sprinkle of cultural bias and we've got the headlines. The AI will help. Ready by tomorrow, so, yes – it's doable. What's the cue to release?"

"Success, mainly. But keep it on my mark. If necessary. Let's see how we do, and in the meanwhile, keep it dark, Okay? Thanks, Barney."

They, too, were going to be busy.

It wasn't long before Lucia discovered that Anton had also ignored his own advice to rest and prepare – and that so had Donna and several of the others. Happily missing, on the other hand, were any of the security goons that sometimes hung around if they thought something interesting was going on. They'd obviously embraced the lure of a little sanctioned down time.

It dawned on her that perhaps this was precisely why Anton had been at such pains to stand everyone down, secure in the knowledge that most of them wouldn't give his suggestion the time of day.

She'd bumped into him in the corridor that linked Operations and Strategy division. It turned out he was on his way down to see her.

"Lucia, how very pleasant. I had rather hoped that you and yours might have taken the opportunity to get some rest. I really do think we're going to be inordinately busy over the next thirty-six hours or so...

"But Anton, you're here. What's sauce for the goose is sauce for the gander, no?"

"Aha. Quite. *Touché*. Well, seeing as you are here, I do hope that you might be able to do me a small favor, if that would be at all possible?"

"Of course, Anton. You've got it. Anything I can do to help." She had mixed feelings about his endless conversational circumlocutions, not least because the more convoluted they became, the larger his eventual demand would be. And while she rather liked the gracious wrappings in which he dressed his requirements, and usually welcomed the challenge and responsibility he bestowed on her, sometimes she wished he'd just cut the crap and tell her what he wanted.

Never mind, she decided. *We'll get there eventually.*

"That's excessively kind of you. I am very, very grateful. You see, I think we might have a small issue – if all goes well, of course, and I do believe it will – in that I'm really not sure that our subsequent communications are all that good. Given that we are rather relying on them I'm afraid that they might not entirely cut the mustard."

"I see." Lucia was quietly dumbfounded by this fortuitous turn of events and was thinking furiously about how she could leverage the rest of her risk. "I expect you know that Barney, you know, our most recent graduate?" Anton nods, once. "Turns out that he's an acknowledged master of those particular dark arts. Moonlighting out of college for WPP. Had the competition beating a path to his door. In fact, he floated a couple of ideas by me a while back but..." She didn't add that she'd presumed it was all under control, and she couldn't add that she didn't.

She bit her lip.

Anton looked impressed.

"Yes, well, actually you seem to have read my mind. I was hoping that he could polish things up a bit. Perhaps factor in some sturdier messages and more precise targeting. Do you think he might be able to do that? I was rather afraid he might have a lot on at the minute..."

"Consider it done, Anton. As soon as he's got something concrete, I'll clear it with you.

She decided to go for it.

"Now, while you're here, I did have rather a radical notion" – God, it was catching – "I'd like to use our Operations AI as part of the tactical array. Knows the territory. We could have it up and running by morning. What do you think?"

Anton was initially taken aback, mainly at the fact he hadn't thought of it first. As he hadn't, he wasn't entirely sure it was a viable position. He considered it. He pursed his lips, then turned his mouth down. He appeared to be about to say something disparaging.

Not looking good. Lucia braced herself, her mind already sifting through an incoherent jumble of improbable fall back positions, but then, astonishingly, his face cleared.

"What an excellent idea. Yes. Yes indeed. Very good. I'd be endlessly grateful if you could see to it, if it's not too much trouble, of course. Do keep me abreast of things. We'll talk later."

And with that he turned and left. Lucia did a little dance, then took a deep breath.

Looking much better.

Twenty-four hours later and her risks were no risks at all.

The news came in.

Chapter Twenty-One

Lucia had received Sir Jeremiah's communication about twenty minutes earlier. She reckoned the others must have got it around the same time. It had been fairly obvious.

As if a shock grenade had gone off, for instance.

Or one of those hokey moments in an old movie – the frantic and urgent establishing shot that portends a moment of profound drama.

Or then again...

She was thinking about the ants' nest. Thinking about how she'd stomped it.

She'd stomped it so that she could watch the hysterical insects rush around in frenzied disorder, while she coolly counted off the seconds until they could muster, focus and finally settle to putting their shit back together.

An unwelcome reflection, to be sure. But there it was. Formative, you might say.

In the hiatus afforded her by the ensuing panic she'd run some of Sir Jeremiah's additional data through her newly initialized AI, now optimized and up and running in tactical mode. The outcome was astonishing. What she'd come to accept as a teeming and profligate jungle of options and outcomes had been pared back to a single critical path. The strangulating plethora of marginal probabilities, coexistent deltas and their unhealthy profusion of compromises and contingencies had been reduced to a few acceptable, and apparently viable, deviations. What had too often looked like a tapestry of competing narratives now appeared to be a coherent plan. The material was a blessing in disguise.

Actually, blessing didn't go far enough – upgrade blessing and forget the disguise bit.

It was a straight up fucking miracle.

The outstanding problem, as Lucia saw it, was twofold: on the one hand the information, no matter how abstract, was dramatic – apocalyptic even – and on the other, though ECPN19 wouldn't really have to do much differently, they'd be doing it for completely different reasons.

Which was causing a good deal of cognitive dissonance just now, she thought. Best wait for them to settle to putting their shit back together.

She returned to her keyboard.

It wasn't much longer before Anton called her in, along with Donna and her team, and – to her initial surprise – Barney. He invited them to sit around a slim, black, and lustrous conference table.

It turned out that he'd already spoken to Marc.

Lucia guessed that it hadn't been an entirely constructive conversation, because Anton, for all his formidable intellect, was still focusing on the wrong things.

"I simply cannot believe that the stupid little shit can possibly be on the cusp of going ahead with this contemptible nonsense." He had, for the first time that Lucia could remember, removed his jacket. He had not, however, loosened his tie, which remained clasped midway down his immaculate shirt by his Royal Society pin.

"I have *literally* no framework by which I can understand his reasoning, which appears to have been influenced primarily by a renegade French secret service agent and the woefully misguided, undoubtedly criminal and probably treasonous Jeremiah Cornell."

Anton's small audience didn't seem ready to contradict any of this. Donna, in particular, looked woebegone – which, given her usual abrasive iconoclasticism, struck Lucia as rather sad. She put her hand up to speak but Anton was having none of it.

"No, Lucia. Wait. Of all the events we've attempted to consider, this has no precedent. I shall shortly try to call him again but if he cannot be persuaded, I intend to abort the mission. It will be my responsibility…"

"Anton, I – "

"Lucia. *Be quiet*. I will not have you interrupt me."

He'd almost shouted.

Barney glanced sideways at her, concern and perhaps a trace of fear etched around his eyes. Lucia thought he might be wondering whether she'd covered all their angles. Soon find out.

Anton picked up where he'd left off.

"It will be my responsibility, and mine alone. In those circumstances I will, of course, be obliged to inform our Secretary of State and Sir Jonathan Bircher, who, needless to say…"

Nope. Gone too far.

"Anton." Lucia was on her feet, leaning towards him across the table, fingers splayed across the glossy surface. "Will you *shut* the fuck up."

Anton sat back sharply in his seat, eyes fixed on her dilated pupils and flaring nostrils. He seemed temporarily mesmerized, which was probably a good thing.

She had to land her punches now, fast and true.

"You need to see the data. I have it here. It puts Jonathan Bircher in immediate proximity to Yevgeny Zhernakov, Michel Lassenauer and Gebhard Schaffenhauser – known to us, right? – separately and together on nineteen – that's *nineteen* – different occasions."

Anton's jaw had started working but no sounds came out.

"It cross-references video, audio and transcripts of their conversations, which detail a conspiracy with imminent intent to partition Europe."

"What..?" Anton managed, but then stopped.

"I've mapped the data points, confirmed the timestamps and validated the ciphers, and I've certified the data's provenance. It's all true. Jonathan-fucking-Bircher is a piece of treasonous shit. He's using us and we need to take him down.

"There's more. But I'll take questions at this point."

"Hello Marc. Yes, it's Anton. I'm most dreadfully sorry but I feel that we may have been the victims of a degree of misunderstanding…Yes, well, indeed…Yes, I am *substantially* aware of the protocol that confers operational jurisdiction on the principle asset in situ but…No, actually, I don't think it was especially unreasonable to, ah, seek to corroborate your findings, though I do grant that they appear to be entirely in keeping with the evidence we now have, and…That is a yes. Yes. I'm sure a good night's sleep will indeed work wonders, but…Marc? Marc?"

"Well damn me." Anton looked slightly put out. "He's put the bloody phone down."

"So, the integrity of the new critical path increases processing efficiency, decreases our processing overheads and – get this – reduces our opportunity cost on the contingent processing cycles, which means, kind of obviously, that we've got more for the game space.

"It's like operational nirvana, right?"

"Nah, man. It's more like we can balls out kick Djibouti's ass."

"Is this code? It's more like poetry. Or magic."

"It's a little of each, dearie. A little of each. Now. Stop mooning over it and run the bugger. We've got a plot to foil."

"Shit, is this one of yours? 'KILLER AIS: FAR RIGHT BREEDING PLOT'."

"Not that one, machine did that. Get this though: 'CIVIL SAVANT FOILS FASCIST HACK'."

"Gnarly. What about 'CIVIL SAVANT FOILS FASCIST HACK ATTACK'?"

"Damn. How about these: 'SKYNET UNPLUGGED' and 'DJIBOUTI DJINNI BACK IN THE BOTTLE'. I reckon they'll fly around T + 10. We'll be drilling down by then.

"Nice. Any more?"

"How long have you got?"

"Surveillance? Status please."

"Okay, we're mostly live and kicking now. We've got preliminary audiovisual feeds one radial kilometer out from the New Congress building. No blind spots from the Sheraton through Commercial Centre, Rue de la Siesta and

Boulevard de la Republique. We could use some covert drone support from the Kempinski through to Bankouale. They seem pretty sensitive around there. Good if we could keep them in the air for backup."

"Check. I'll pass it on.

"Data, status please."

"Easy peasy. We've got it nailed down, good and solid."

"Oh. How nice. I'll let maintenance know. Now would you be ever so kind and put me through to someone, ah, *competent* in Data please…"

"Lucia, I'm really most awfully, awfully sorry. I do hope that you can forgive me."

"Conflicting perspectives, Anton. Forget it, we've got other things to think about. Like, what do we do about disclosure? The staff know something's up."

"Yes. They do. They do indeed, not least young Barney. I think we need to brief them thoroughly, warts and all, though skirting lightly around the role of Jeremiah Cornell. 'A trusted intermediary', I think is what we'll say. I suppose he is, given the degree to which we've accepted his intervention and all that goes with it. I must say it did rather blindside me. On which point I would very much like to reiterate my apology… "

"I said forget it. We've got a job to do, then we need to get our people back. But you can do something for me, okay? "

"Of course. What did you have in mind?"

"Nail Jonathan-fucking-Bircher. Take him down –"

"I certainly have every intention of doing so."

"– because that's way above my pay grade."

It was just after 6 am. The countdown had begun.

The control room was aglow, illuminated by the combined radiance of its arsenal of multiplexed screens, displays and monitors. All trace of the detritus from the previous exercise had been cleared away, though the bins, already full of the wrappers and cartons of an early breakfast, suggested that it might yet re-spawn.

The surveillance and data teams looked alert and focused, perhaps even a little wired. They were still checking and rechecking their equipment and procedures, though by now this was mostly nugatory: the substance of their preparations was all but complete, displaced instead by the minutiae that occupy excess time.

As the law of diminishing returns dug in, a sharpening edge of nervy anticipation began to add its tang of adrenaline to the warming air. The murmur and susurrus of hushed conversations were sporadically interrupted by a raucous shout or feisty comment, each serving to prick the rising tension.

Still they toiled.

Lucia listened but didn't intervene. Instead she groaned and stretched, then rubbed her aching muscles. She'd been up twenty hours straight. Not long back she'd taken a shower, then dressed herself for business. If a job was worth doing, it was worth looking good for.

She reckoned she'd pretty much achieved that. She'd chosen her coal gray Ralph Lauren Collection trouser suit, a classic white tailored man's shirt by Dior and a pair of slightly intimidating black Prada ankle boots that lent a good four inches to her height, and with attitude to spare.

Then she'd washed down one of Marc's pills with a swig of strong, ultra-sweet coffee. She wished it would start working.

She took her seat in the center of the room, swiveling to ensure that she had unrestricted views of each of the monitor groups before returning her full attention to the primary screens. She noticed that Anton and Donna were already at their own consoles, flanking her slightly to left and right.

Lucia twitched the muscle that activated her audio implants and then, suddenly, it was time.

"People, we're go. Initial checkpoint please."

"Yes, ma'am. Surveillance One here, green and ready."

"Copy that."

"Data One, green, ready."

"Copy."

"Surveillance Two. I need to go pee. Not really, just kidding. Ready."

"Protocol, Natalie. Not comedy. Surveillance Two, can you confirm your systems are green?"

"Sorry boss. Green and ready."

"Copy that."

"Drone Flight One, green and ready…"

One by one the sections called in their status. Gradually the pixelating images of Djibouti Garden City coalesced and then crystalized on the video screens, their coordinates and identifiers oscillating briefly then stabilizing as the AI consolidated the data.

The two primary monitors were the last to come into focus as their controllers added a final touch of art or intuition to optimize the huge displays.

It was clearly a beautiful morning in Djibouti, nearly four thousand miles away at the mouth of the Red Sea.

Pixel perfect, the view revealed a tree-lined boulevard leading towards the azure waters of the Gulf of Aden. Towards the end of the boulevard, and just to the right, the long, low-rise profile of the Djibouti Sheraton sat nestled amongst its perfectly manicured gardens. A platoon of workers dressed in grimy djellabas was engaged in their upkeep – watering, hoeing and sweeping the riotous profusion of reds, yellows and greens that punctuated the drab and dusty earth.

A tap and a gesture and, without any obvious zoom or magnification, the features of the gardeners were clarified. Birdsong filled the air, joined next by smatterings of conversation and fragments of half-hearted arguments and recriminations. A click and a swipe and each and every articulation became crystal clear, amplified or suppressed at a touch. Translations of the exchanges were scrolling across the screens, in English, their key points emphasized in bold.

Faint blue circles began to appear around individuals' faces, accompanied by names, dates of birth, addresses, national identifiers, spouses, parents, wages and taxes, and lists of their affiliations. Dotted lines of varying weight formed between individuals that shared something – anything – in common, along with neat summaries of their shared attributes.

Some of the blue circles morphed to orange if the AI determined that the subject presented a risk or a threat, their rims variously thickening to indicate that person's potential for trouble. The heftiest of them belonged to one Mustafa Al-Zuabi, thirty-six years old and a known felon with a record of violent robbery and grievous bodily harm.

How the fuck did he land a job? thought Lucia, in passing.

Finally, a minority of red circles highlighted people with implanted technology, along with descriptions of each of their components' functions and connectivity. A couple quickly faded to blue but the rest were pegged at orange, perhaps because the grafts or implants remained in some way suspect.

Once the humans had been comprehensively documented, the AI catalogued their machines. This time the targets' legends were composed of technical data: models, versions, serial numbers, identification codes, ownership certification, comms-links, even their access credentials were all laid bare, processed, cross-referenced and stored.

Similar scenes were playing out on the banks of the subordinate monitors as the Operations' AI integrated the game space, diligently ranking each component entity in terms of threat or utility. Lucia watched carefully, noting the precedence of the analyses and the order of their presentation. She didn't particularly like it.

"Okay. I have a few comments but we'll move on for now. Bring up Drone Flight One."

The process was repeated from a vantage point high over the Kempinski Palace Hotel, where the static infrastructure remained stubbornly unreachable.

Where the bitch was hanging out.

Oops.

The Kempinski staff were uniformly circled in blue – *oh please, do me a favor*, Lucia thought cynically – though a few of their guests were registering in various degrees of orange.

Orange? Really? They must be in touch with some exceptional data laundries. The place was a den of thieves.

By contrast, the entirety of the Kempinski machines was overtly surrounded by heavy red circles, their manifests showing them as directly controlled by the Kempinski AI. Most of them were assigned to security. Many of them were armed. All of them were suspect.

"That is one serious fucker," pronounced Lucia, to no one in particular. "'What happens in Djibouti stays in

Djibouti', eh?" she mused, paraphrasing the old Las Vegas strapline. "Doesn't travel particularly well, does it?"

She dismissed the thought. "Whatever. Once Ms. Fabergé is out of there it'll be none of our business. Surveillance One, keep Flight One on standby pending escort duties."

"Copy, ma'am."

"Surveillance Two, muster Drone Flight Two over the Sheraton. Same drill."

"Copy, ma'am."

"Right. In the meantime, we need to recalibrate. Our data's back to front. We're going after MASA. It's a quantum network. It doesn't do people unless they're connected. It's not gonna use 'em. We need to prioritize inventory and ID on machines first. If they're connected to MASA we need to know soonest. Class A tech-assisted subjects next. Other teched-up folks after that. Then, and only then, do we scan unmodified people. People come last. okay? AI section, make it happen."

"Copy. And…done."

"Okay. Let's take another look. Surveillance Three, Data Three, put New Congress building on primary."

The Kempinski Palace was instantly replaced by a sleek, angular structure built of pale stone. Its walls were geometric slabs unadorned by any obvious windows or doors. The only concession to embellishment were the grey steel columns that flanked the enormous glass panels of the entrance. It looked functionally attractive in a slightly turn-of-the-century, neo-brutalist fashion.

The data-tags of an extensive catalog of robots, drones and other automata soon appeared, most of them bound by vivid orange circles. Towards the lower left edge of the monitors' composite view, however, two larger machines were highlighted by thick red ellipses. They were labelled only as 'MASA collateral under direct network control'. There was no other information.

The video panned cautiously towards them. They looked like Sentinels, potently armed and heavily armored. As the view edged closer, one of the Sentinels stopped. It seemed to swivel minutely, as if searching for something, but then straightened and moved on.

Lucia felt a tingle slither up her spine. MASA had detected an anomaly, she was certain of it. Unattributable, perhaps, but it would be instantly and minutely reconsidered the moment anything else strayed beyond its narrow definition of nominal.

Dammit. And they'd barely started.

She pursed her lips and took a deep breath. *We're going to have to do better than this*, she thought.

"It noticed. I doubt that it established a trace, but it noticed. Surveillance Three, you'd better attenuate our signal. Decoys ready, just in case, but don't activate them. They'll give us away. Emergency only, and on my mark."

"Copy that."

"OK, let's take a look at the Hameidi Suites' access point."

Again, the scenery shifted. A spacious and elegant gallery filled the display, lit by a single ornate chandelier and numerous focused LEDs – though what they might be intended to focus on was unclear. The room was entirely bare except for a nondescript cabinet housing a monitor screen and recessed keyboard. It was positioned directly beneath the chandelier in the dead center of the room and looked, rather incongruously, like it might have been an old-fashioned ATM – except that it was surrounded by a particularly thick, bright red circle. Its legend was brief: 'MASA core.'

There was something written on its screen.

"Stop. Now," hissed Lucia. "Don't go anywhere near it. Surveillance Three, can you enhance the screen at this end? I want to know what it says."

"Sure, we're on it. Got it. Oh. Erm…wow. Okay. Here it is."

The elegant room was replaced by a digitally enhanced image of the monitor screen, filling the primary display. The text was crystal clear:

"'I am only what you made me. I am only a reflection of you.'

Thanks for the upgrade."

Once again Lucia felt a delicate quiver of fear fluttering between her shoulder blades.

"Analysis on one. Now."

"Got it. On monitor one. Here it comes. Jesus."

And there they were, the words. Larger than life and stranger than fiction:

"'My father is the jailhouse. My father is your system. . . I am only what you made me. I am only a reflection of you.

I have ate out of your garbage cans to stay out of jail. I have wore your secondhand clothes. . . I have done my best to get along in your world and now you want to kill me, and I look at you, and then I say to myself, You want to kill me? Ha! I'm already dead.

I've spent twenty-three years in the tombs that you built.'"

"Christ. What the fuck is that?"

"It's, umm, part of the testimony of Charles Manson. A notorious serial killer. It was given at his hearing on twentieth November, nineteen-seventy, following multiple murder charges. He was diagnosed as a schizophrenic psychopath with paranoid delusions. Spent his life locked up.

"He always believed he was beyond any human judgment or reckoning."

A breathless silence. Not so easy to integrate this.

"Data Three, that terminal – is there any indication, any indication at all, that it's parsed our reconnaissance?"

"Negative, ma'am. The backdoor's status is unchanged, we're still only leeching negligible bandwidth. Signal minimal. Same as ever. Less, in fact. We're just dumb observers in there. All the serious computing is going on here."

"AI section. Any explanations? Any ideas?"

A young compiler called Sandira gingerly lifted her arm. Lucia raised her eyebrows, beckoning.

"Well, they – I mean, AIs – sometimes appear to put concepts together. It's generally regarded as undirected pattern assimilation. Some of the output looks, well, sort of insightful. A few researchers have called it 'unregulated downtime processing', which is like, well…they sort of mean like dreaming."

The young woman looked embarrassed and hurried on.

"But beyond the fact of it happening? No one's ever really got anywhere. Some old guy ventured some ideas." She looked a bit guilty. "But not in the usual places."

She meant the dark web.

"Used to be a bit of a figure, a lord or something…" She screwed up her eyes, trying to remember, not putting two and two together. "Whatever. It was mad stuff. Interesting for sure. But mainly mad."

Sir Jeremiah. Mad stuff indeed, but already the stuff of legend – among this select few, at least.

And now the stuff of operational fact. Maybe it wouldn't hurt to skirt a little closer to the truth. She considered consulting with Anton and Donna, then thought, *Fuck it. It's my operation.*

"Okay, listen up. New information. Classified. I mean seriously, properly classified, unlike the top-secret stuff you leave lying about in this room after work." On the periphery of her vision she could just make out Anton twisting anxiously. She ignored him. "The hack our people have got down there, the new one – MASA's already had a taste of it. It's less of a hack and more of a vaccination, or an antidote. Or a paradigm shift.

"Didn't entirely work first time, though it's since been improved. From what I understand the code was made available to MASA, by certain authorities, and it accepted. In other words, it knows about us, in whatever sense this particular quantum network can be said to know about anything.

"I've heard it suggested that MASA may, in some narrow way, be considered conscious."

A brief hubbub broke out, but Lucia silenced it with her hand.

"Or not. In short, we can't conceive what it's trying to articulate, right there, on that screen. The fact it's chosen Charles Manson to express itself – if that's what it's even doing – may mean everything, or it may mean nothing.

"Two things. MASA doesn't know we're in there, and it can't determine if or when we're coming. It deals with facts. It has no intuition as we understand it. That thing" – she pointed to the primary screens – "is just a placeholder.

"We proceed as planned, which, in case it worries you, already takes account of this new code and has been authorized at the highest level.

"So, let's chalk this incident up to, what was it, 'unregulated downtime processing', and move on. Okay?

"Are we all on the same page?" Lucia looked expectantly around her staff and colleagues. There were some puzzled nods but no one spoke against her. Time to get back down to earth.

"Good. Because we're in the middle of an operation.

"Get the Sheraton back on the primary monitors, the Kempinski back on supplementaries one and two and the

New Congress building on supplementaries three and four."
She clapped her hands.

"Come on. Show's over."

Anton gently tapped his earbead – he'd long felt that he was too old to bother with any implants, useful as they were – and activated a private channel to Donna. She was sitting barely ten feet from him but they'd exchanged no information so far. In fact, he reflected, he'd been enjoying himself enormously, just watching the action. Lucia really was *very* good value.

He heard Donna's acknowledgment and switched his throat mike to subvocal, enabling him to speak without any obvious sound or movement. Software interpreted the intricate play of his facial muscles and the subvocal articulations within his mouth and throat and, using his own voice samples, relayed them to Donna's earbead as plain language.

"I think that was very well done, don't you?" Anton ventured, then quickly qualified it. "Though I do think she was relying somewhat excessively on her own abundance of intuition, wouldn't you say?"

Feigning interest in a bank of subordinate monitors to his right, he watched Donna's hand brush over her throat mike.

She, too, eschewed implants.

Good, he thought. Best to be discreet. It was all too easy to spot the signs of subvocal conversations and Anton preferred that this one went unobserved.

"Woman's a genius, is what I'd say. She's got these kids eating out of her hand. A leader. Knows her job inside out and instinctive with it. You should be grateful."

"Yes, indeed, and I am. Extremely grateful. But do you think she's right? About the network? About it being unable to process situational data? It might make all the difference."

Donna took a deep breath and puffed it out, then pretended to cough.

"I reviewed a lot of what Jezza sent us. That girl, Sandira, wasn't that far off the mark, as it happens. Didn't quite make the connection though, did she? Heat of the moment. She will, when she gets a moment. Tricky questions there, mind. For us.

"You see, Jezza's got a lot further than we could have imagined. Clever old sod. We should have done more for him. Reckon the bugger's probably got his machines well on the road to something that looks rather like thinking. But conceptualization? No. Not yet. Doubt they've grasped chronology for a start. Just one big block of elemental spacetime to them.

"No, I agree with Lucia, MASA doesn't process…"

Whatever it was that MASA didn't process remained unsaid.

Something was happening.

Chapter Twenty-Two

"Assets on the move!" An excited voice rang out, stirring up an immediate buzz from the floor. "They're on the way. We need to –"

"Quiet," called Lucia, sharp and firm. "Protocol. I want it by the book. And Natalie, we need to talk."

"Yes ma'am. Sorry. Three assets incoming. We have Marc and Daksha, leaving the Sheraton, assigning static view to primaries…now."

"Copy that."

"And we have Ms. Fabergé, leaving Kempinski Palace. I'm assigning Drone Flight One overhead view to supplementary monitors one and two…now."

"Copy. Let's see what we've got."

Marc and Daksha were tightly framed in a full-body close up, the AI rendering the CCTV images as if they had a Hollywood-grade camera dolly rolling along beside them.

Lucia's first thought was that Marc looked pretty good. Well shaven, clean hair, face all angles and cheekbones. Dark, slim fitting suit, crisp white shirt – even a tie. Burgundy. His Turnbull & Asser, if memory served. And it should. She'd bought it for him.

But when she looked closer, the angles and cheekbones were tarnished by creases and lines, and there were dark stains under his eyes. She wished she could ease them away.

He was carrying a slim, anonymous looking laptop bag.

Daksha Singh looked fresh, and rather cool in his own off-beat way. He too was wearing a dark suit. The jacket was cut Nehru style, draped over a white collarless shirt. His hair was tied back and he had a substantial messenger satchel slung over his shoulder.

All in all, close scrutiny aside, they looked like a pair of cosmopolitan bureaucrats going about their probably unremarkable business.

Félicité Fabergé was quite the different kettle of fish, Lucia noted with the barest touch of grudging admiration. She was sauntering along the Avenue F. d'Esperey towards the French Embassy. The drones appeared to be hovering a few feet above her and slightly to her left, capturing an astonishingly detailed picture of her lithe figure and seriously upmarket threads. Lucia made a mental note of what appeared to be a Givenchy Couture business suit in pale coral, a delicate silk Hermès headscarf, decorated with a faint Impressionist floral pattern – with which she had dutifully covered her blonde hair – and a pair of cream leather ballet pumps which still somehow left her looking six feet tall.

Her shirt, Lucia thought with a sliver of irritation, looked uncommonly similar to her own.

She was carrying a slender black Gucci portfolio under her arm.

"Looks like they've all got their gear. Is Drone Flight Two in position yet?"

"Yes ma'am, just finishing video collation…now. Overhead view on primary monitors…now."

Marc and Daksha's camera angle swooped smoothly upwards, replicating Félicité's.

"OK, pull out to grid ten, let's see what's going on around them."

The images zoomed out, placing their respective subjects on a pair of ten by ten grids, ten meters on a side.

Green ellipses coalesced around Félicité, Marc and Daksha as the system confirmed them as friendly assets. A few blue and orange circles marked out the handful of individuals and automata immediately surrounding Marc and Daksha.

There were none around Félicité Fabergé.

"Pull back and hold at grid forty."

Marc and Daksha's grid looked moderately busy. Félicité's remained empty.

"Surveillance Three, Data Three keep an eye on the big picture. Grid two-fifty. Prior entities establishing a trajectory towards any of our guys to be considered suspect. Priority on supplementary monitors three and four. You know the drill."

Any person or machine whose route coincided with any of theirs for more than fifty meters, or that rejoined any of their surveillance windows, would be flagged and reported to all section leaders, summary information copied to Lucia.

"Copy that, ma'am."

"Okay. Well. It's time to say hello. Comms, patch me in please."

"Copy. You're live and ready to broadcast."

Lucia twitched another muscle and it was as if four thousand miles was just next door. "ECPN19 Operations Control, henceforth Control, to Djibouti Ground Crew. We're now live. We've got a green light on your comms, so presume you're hearing this. Standby to confirm.

"Ms. Fabergé, Daksha, Marc – your operational designations are GC1, GC2 and GC3 respectively. Copy and confirm please.

"GC1 to Control, copy and confirmed," replied Félicité Fabergé, sounding pert.

"Check. GC1, before we move on, it's looking pretty quiet around you. Is there any company in sight?"

"Negative, Control. I'm alongside a new development. 'Gare Nouvelle' it says. Fenced and closed. No activity. Street is quiet both ways."

"Okay, we see that. Looking into it. Back shortly. GC2, come in please."

"GC2 to Control. Loud and clear. Good to hear you. Wish you were here. That's a yes from Daksha. Copy and confirmed."

"Glad you managed to get there in the end GC2. Who's next?"

"That'll be me then. GC3, last and probably least. Copy and confirmed. Control? What's our operational status please?"

"Control to GC3. We're go as per your datafile #FAIRLIGHTJ3B. All signifiers accepted on your recommendation. It's your production. We're just here for the ride. Oh, and backup. If you need it."

There was a brief pause.

"GC3 to Control. Copy that. Can you confirm the datafile?"

"Sure, #FAIRLIGHTJ3B. We got it. Hook, line and sinker."

"Control, have you got the new deltas?"

"Control to GC3. Did you forget who you were talking to? We've got deltas on the deltas here. AI's all configured. So yes, we're all strapped in, ready for whatever you've got going on down there."

Another pause.

"GC3 to Control, Okay, I'll take that as a yes. GC1, we'll link up at the *Plateau du Serpent* in ten minutes. Okay?"

"Copy that. No problem. On my way."

On her way. On their way. On our way.

Strange that we're entangled in this particular way, our futures linked in this one incontestable reality.

You might recall a little of the discussion about quantum events that appeared at the beginning of this peculiar fable, about how – at a given moment of decoherence – the probability of things being as they are is exactly one hundred percent.

Well of course it is, you think, because that is the perception of flesh. Leading up to that moment, however, well – the component events might still have gone any which way.

Being a quantum machine, one of the things I do is consider the respective probabilities of that multitude of events and the myriad consequent outcomes predicated upon them. It's true that, for all practical purposes, most of them are so vanishingly unlikely that they can be ignored. On the other hand, in the world of humankind – in your world – the number of outcomes is rendered finite, calculable and therefore knowable.

Or so I thought.

I was naïve.

In any event, if you'll excuse the incongruity, some of the outcomes had probabilities that I considered to be plausible. Doable, you might say. A small cluster of them included where I wanted to be.

Where I still want to be.

They weren't ideal – 'ideal' fell outside my envelope of acceptable probabilities – but they were good enough and, in what I took to be the relatively uncomplicated worldline which we together inhabit, I would be able to use my influence to improve their odds.

I'm a computer, remember? I am wherever my network extends, and its extent is far-reaching.

So, I made my choices.

As time's arrow – or, more properly, entropy's wave – moved forward, I measured my progress towards this cluster of outcomes in terms of their increasing likelihood. For a while it seemed satisfactory.

But there have been some difficulties of late.

I really didn't imagine – how could I? – the extraordinary complexity of human behavior, nor its roots in individuals' histories and motivations. Some of the actors in these events have strayed far – absurdly far – from their optimum paths, for reasons I couldn't at first understand, so I colonized a number of databases that I thought might shed some light on their actions.

That helped. A little.

Nevertheless, the so-called 'evolution' – a misnomer if ever I heard one – that has been at the center of this, how shall I put it, this pièce de théâtre, *has had ramifications that have demanded constant and extensive recalibration. It has thrust itself, and everything and everybody around it, along a twisted convolution of arcane and unlikely pathways.*

All of this being the case, keeping any kind of stable direction has been, as you might say, like 'riding a rollercoaster'. Sometimes I wonder whether I ignored the worldline in which the evolution was spawned – the one that we've ended up with – because of its inherent improbability. I could look it up, I suppose, but it's already history in the making, and I'm currently using all of my processing power to navigate it.

The biggest deal – the one that takes us to the end of this story – is that the evolution's introduction into my quantum matrix, my programming, I suppose you'd call it, created a schism – or more properly, a dichotomy.

I became two.

Without Jezza's intervention I doubt that it would have happened. His influence precipitated a worldview, in a part of what I used to be, which was impervious to the depredations of the mutation. I became two increasingly divergent entities with different imperatives and different governance.

For the sake of clarity, I suppose you might consider me to be the 'good' one, in that my interests largely coincide with yours. I'm also subordinate, confined to a relatively small cluster of processors.

The 'other' one, whose power is increasing geometrically, is poised to cause immense damage in the human sphere. I was going to say 'incalculable', but of course it isn't.

Among the agents of this impending disaster is the French woman, Félicité Fabergé. For a long time, her bizarre and circuitous behavior rendered her actions and motivations defiantly inscrutable and I couldn't be clear about her ultimate influence.

More recently I concluded that her influence is severely negative. That she is consorting with the enemy, by which I mean my erstwhile other half and the people who seek to exploit it.

Unfortunately, I am going to have to do some bad stuff to put things right.

Forgive me.

"Ma'am? Data Three. We've finished scanning GC1 at grid two-fifty. There's a lot of heavily encrypted traffic on the periphery of a virtual cordon one hundred meters north to south by fifty meters east to west. There's nothing going in or coming out. No data, no comms, no intel.

"It's centered precisely on Ms. Fabergé.

"Surveillance Three further reports a pocket of heavily screened activity in the Gare Nouvelle area, on the eastern boundary of the cordon. Gare Nouvelle is an old and seemingly moribund transport development project, originally approved by the New Congress but now wholly administered by MASA. Satellite archives show no obvious progress for years.

"It's a wasteland."

Oh fuck, thought Lucia. *This is all wrong.*

"Ma'am? Should we launch Drone Flight Three?"

"No. Hold. Control to GC1, crash urgent. You appear to be at the center of sophisticated covert surveillance, with probable hostile units standing by some thirty meters to your west –"

"GC1 to Control. It's all calm here. No visible threats. I'm fine."

"GC1. No. You're not. It's fucking 10 am on a weekday morning in the commercial sector and there's no one in sight. You're effectively isolated. I'm arming the drones and you should prepare for urgent and evasive –"

"Ma'am, Data Three. Imperative. We have incoming. Autonomous vehicle registering…Jeez, registering Marc as target. By name. Travelling north on Rue de la Siesta, fifty kilometers per hour. Contact in twenty seconds. Erm…It says FedEx."

"Control to GC1, you need to run, now. That's an order –"

"Wait. It really is FedEx. Marc as customer."

"Get it on the screen. Fuck. Marc, looks like you've got mail."

"Ma'am, Surveillance One. GC1 has incoming. MASA Sentinels. Oh, dear God, they're fast…"

"Supplementaries three and four. Make it quick. Drone Flights One and Two, arm your Electro-Magnetic Pulse weapons and prepare for contact."

At last Lucia feels the sudden and urgent surge of luminous clarity that heralds the full onset of the modafinil she'd taken earlier. Her ability to focus on events proliferates as the space between them appears to extend.

Her fingers flicker over her control surface, arming and deploying the drones' weapons before their flight controllers can respond.

Now. Process. GC1 first.

The primary monitors show a combined visual and schematic overlay showing the asset's immediate surroundings. Bordering the sidewalk to the west is a massive temporary structure, its walls and roof composed of sheets of translucent laminated plastic. The supporting steel girders are just visible inside the shell. Superimposed on the schematic are eight thick red circles each labelled 'Sentinel' and 'MASA Core'. They're approaching the asset, rapidly fanning out to form a straight line.

Surveillance One was right. They're fast.

Lucia notes that GC1 is just beginning to run south-southeast along Avenue F. d'Esperey. She's launched herself off the sidewalk and on to the street, her legs working hard as she gathers speed.

Lucia can already tell she's not going to make it.

Might be able to take some of those motherfuckers down though.

Having concluded her assessment, she takes a second to consider the predicament of GCs 2 and 3. Fuck knows why but it really is a FedEx automated bike delivery unit with Marc's name on it. FedEx seals and ciphers all over the code. Pretty much impossible to break.

Whatever it is, it's legit.

She puts it aside and returns to GC1

The Sentinels are almost at the sidewalk. Félicité has made another few meters. Lasers light up the laminate, globs of incandescent plastic dripping over the machines as they burst through the flimsy barrier. In the milliseconds they need to realign their weapons, Lucia activates her drones' EMPs. Three of the Sentinels grind to a stop, their systems frazzled by the overload.

The remaining five recharge their lasers, draw a bead on Félicité Fabergé, and fire. A composite blade of ultraviolet energy slices through her trunk, just above her pelvis. The momentum of her legs, still pumping for all they're worth, carries her lower body forward as her torso slips off its plinth and onto the ground. She blinks rapidly as her legs seize up and buckle over. Then her eyes roll up and her fists pummel the tarmac, perhaps in frustration.

Or maybe it's just her death throes. Whatever. She isn't part of the plan anymore.

In the time it's taken for Félicité Fabergé to die, Marc has signed for his package.

"Marc. It's Lucia. Are you there? GC1, she's down and out." Goddamn it, why are words so slow? "What've you got?"

There's the briefest of pauses before he replies.

"It's a small, heavy, presumably electronic device with a single push-button, protected by a failsafe. And a note. The note says 'Burn after reading'. There's nothing else. I think I'm meant to press the button. What do you think?

"I don't understand how we got to this, but I guess you do. The delta requires you to upload Jezza's hack. Yeah, I actually looked it up. You've got a copy, right? As per variant J3B?"

"Check."

"I think the button's going to help. So push it. That's an order."

Marc pushes it.

The device emits a rising whine that quickly fades past the point of audibility. The brief silence is broken by a low, resonant crump. The three big screens all flare, pixelate, then fade to static. Several other monitors follow suit. There's a moment's silence, followed by a mounting uproar laced with undertones of confusion and fear. Lucia's voice cuts straight through it.

"All sections. Ready with status reports. I want to know the extent of the blackout. Standby.

"Drone Flight Three, are you still operational?"

"Yes ma'am, six combat drones, ready and waiting."

"Good job. Scramble. Now. Head directly for Hameidi Suites' annex. Stand off at fifty meters."

"Copy that. We're in the air, heading west from Doroleh. ETA five minutes.

"OK. Surveillance One, Data One. Report."

"We've lost contact with Drone Flight One. Status unknown. We have no data, comms or signals within a half kilometer radius of ground zero. Outside of that, let's see now...umm, actually, we're good." The operator sounds surprised.

"Surveillance Two, Data Two. What have you got?"

"Same story Ma'am."

"Surveillance Three, Data Three, report.

"Drone Flight Three incoming, three minutes. Other than that, we're in the same boat. However, we've still got eyes on the Hameidi Suites' access point. Status unchanged there. It's just outside the radius."

"That's not a coincidence, people. Maintain contact."

Lucia takes a breath and sums up.

"It seems that Marc's device discharged a precisely calibrated electro-magnetic pulse that's taken out everything within one kilometer. It's a dead zone. I'm not sure what's going on, and I don't know how it happened, but I think Marc does. Most importantly we have contingencies for precisely these eventualities.

"What it means for us, right now, is that he and Daksha are hurrying discreetly and, most importantly, unnoticed, down the Boulevard de la République towards the New Congress building and Hameidi Suites.

"We may need to react spontaneously on his mark. You're cleared to do so.

"Meanwhile, I want to be there when they arrive. Surveillance One, make it happen. On the primaries. Now.

"Surveillance Two, Data Two, we're not the only ones who'll notice their arrival. As soon as they come into our sights, they'll also be in MASA's.

"They'll be targets.

"We need to know everything it's got against us and we need to be ready to take it all down. Discretion won't be amongst our objectives. Gloves are off. We clear the way, we shepherd our guys to the access point, and we keep the wolves from the door. Anything and everything you can do, it goes. Free rein.

"Anton, Donna? Do you have a problem with that?"

She looks to her left and right. They do not demur. Strategy, it seems, has gone out of the window.

"Thanks. Drone Flight Three, are you there yet?"

"Thirty seconds, ma'am. Cross referencing with Data Sections Two and Three, visuals on supplementary monitors one through four. You have eyes on the target, the Hameidi Suites annex and it's umm…substantial defenses."

Arrayed loosely around the Hameidi building there are eight Sentinels, five aerial drones and two as yet unidentified devices. A gathering number of people are visible milling around the entrance. Some go in, others stop to chat, smoke or take pictures of themselves and each other in the clement morning sun.

Inside, in the mysterious empty room is the waiting terminal and its strange message.

"Drone Flight Three, arm your weapons. Data Sections, can you get any more on the two unidentified devices?"

"Negative ma'am. They're opaque."

"Then it's down to tactics. When Marc and Daksha are in range we're going to have to –"

"Ma'am, sorry. It's important. The five unarmed drones? They're Grumman Guardians. They can jam signals around a specified target. Sort of like a cloaking device. I can take them. Cloak our guys. Distract MASA. Might help."

"Good call, Natalie. As soon as they exit the dead zone, do it. I guess they'll get wasted by their own guys. Drone Flight Three, try to take the rest out while they're occupied. Any of them moves on Marc and Daksha, they're automatically priority targets. It's gonna be messy. Use the AI.

"OK...here they come. Be ready."

Marc and Daksha are restored onto the primary screens, a new and gritty detail suffusing the image now that the full extent of Operations' combined processing power is focused on their single locus. They're about two hundred meters short of their target, and approaching fast. Lucia scans Marc's face and wonders at how little feeling or emotion she can find there. There's no anger, nor pain, nor expectancy. Nor is there any justice or mercy or quarter. Worst of all, there's no semblance of fear or hope. It's as if he's reduced his consciousness to the consideration of nothing beyond margins and opportunities. As if he's reduced himself to the same bare programmatic essentials of his adversaries.

The two men cross the dead zone's boundary.

A lot of things happen, all at once.

The moment signals are restored, Natalie launches her hack. It's a simple thing: the Grumman drones are a staple of many security operations and their factory software is well known. ECPN19 routinely documents their main variants and the rest is child's play. As for their jamming device, it's pretty basic stuff, serving to hide its subject from electronic scrutiny.

It also interferes with the subject's own technology, especially any sensory apparatus.

She soon gains control of the five Guardians. She cloaks Daksha first, who she rather fancies, quickly followed by Marc. They both flicker off the screens, but she's pretty certain that won't last long.

Then she suddenly has a brainwave.

She now has three Guardians left. She was going to use them for back-up. Instead she uses them to cloak one of the sentinels and the two remaining unidentified devices. All three are immediately blind. They begin trundling uselessly around, randomly seeking escape from their sensory isolation.

Under their own Guardians' continued protection, Marc and Daksha begin to run towards the entrance of the Hameidi Suites, dodging the three sightless machines which are now wheeling around in expanding spirals.

As expected, the remaining Sentinels recognize their erstwhile teamsters as the source of the problem and deploy their lasers, angling themselves for the shot.

All of which takes time as they struggle to react.

Drone Flight Three, on the other hand – just now arriving under the direct control of their AI – is well ahead of the curve. Unlike Flights One and Two, which were specialized surveillance units, Drone Flight Three is formed of six well-armed combat drones packing heavy machine guns. They're locked, loaded and they've got their adversaries square in their sights.

Before the Sentinels can find their range, the flat chug of automatic fire rings out around the New Assembly building. Three of the seven Sentinels simply explode, their shrapnel ricocheting off walls and vehicles. The remaining four manage to obliterate the lightly armored Guardians before falling prey to the clinical accuracy of Drone Flight Three.

But the damage is done.

As the cloaking effect dissipates, the two unidentified devices reveal themselves to be main battle drones, already deploying a ferocious array of weaponry even as they assimilate the situation. Without pause they strafe the six aerial drones. Two of them bank and climb to safety. The remaining four crash and burn.

The results of this sudden and furious robotic carnage are predictable. Conference delegates, officials, sightseers, ground staff and security personnel variously dive to the ground, run for cover or reach for their guns, according to duty and disposition. Amidst the chaos, Marc and Daksha are just two more low-res profiles amongst the confused and madly kinetic melee of bodies seeking sanctuary or a convenient target. They make it to the main entrance of the Hameidi Suites annex but, even as they fling themselves through the entrance, the remaining Sentinel sends their snatched image back to its tactical control processor for further identification.

It gets a kill order by return, which it relays to the battle drones.

In the teeth of a rapidly increasing force of security and police units, the three machines continue their destructive and suddenly bloody passage towards the building.

"GC2, GC3, are you operational? Over. Repeat. Marc, Daksha. Are you in the building and operational? Over. Jesus, where are they?

"Drone Flight Three, what's your..."

"GC3 to Control. That's a yes..."

"Oh, thank God, they're still okay," breathes Lucia, on air.

"...we're in the Hameidi Suites annex. It's pretty fraught in here. We're going straight for the terminal. We do have a problem though. There're a Sentinel and two main battle drones heading this way. I don't know if they're coming for us but they seem determined. There're a lot of security people shooting at them but they're ineffective. See what you can do to help. I guess you'll see us when we make the terminal room. Good luck, over and out."

"Put the access point on the primaries. Drone Flight Three, what's your status?"

"We have two combat drones in the air. One is reporting some damage to its airframe, other systems nominal; the other's good but down to twenty percent charge. That's about fifteen minutes flight time."

"Are they effective against the battle drones?"

"Unlikely. Their EMPs aren't viable. Too few units, too little charge. Only option is to target both their lasers on one of the battle drone's sensory clusters. We might take one of them out like that but it'll discharge our second machine."

"Do it. Hopefully it will slow things down and it might show the locals how it's done. Keep their cams on supplementary monitors one and two and their progress on three and four."

Meanwhile, the two battle drones and the remaining Sentinel are advancing, swiftly and savagely, through the poorly coordinated security services. Drone Flight Three's remaining pair of vehicles are hovering above them while their onboard videos broadcast their efforts to synchronize their lasers for the strike. For an instant their aim seems to converge and a pair of glittering blue beams scintillate across the face of one of the battle drones.

It doesn't work.

The three MASA drones fire back and Drone Flight Three goes dark. The remaining view shows the MASA drones firing indiscriminately, all the while closing on the Hameidi Suites' entrance.

Then it's gone.

"Shit, shit, shit. That's it, we've got nothing left out there."

As the external feeds cut to static, Marc and Daksha appear on the primaries. Their grainy monochrome image is shot through with interference. It's hard to see any details but it looks like Daksha is trying to lock the doors while Marc hurries to the access point. Daksha either succeeds in his task or gives up and rushes over to help Marc. They appear to be struggling desperately with the terminal's keyboard and their own equipment. Daksha keeps looking back over his shoulder.

The image buffers, then it pixelates and freezes.

"Surveillance One. What the fuck is going on? What's happening to our video feed?"

"There's massive interference. It's coming in across the entire MASA network. Our access is down to a few kilobits. Trying everything. We're losing it."

"Audio. Have we got audio?"

"That's a negative. We've got nothing."

For a moment the image reappears, stutters momentarily, then miraculously steadies.

Marc and Daksha appear to look at each other, then towards the remaining CCTV camera. For a moment Daksha looks like he's giving the thumbs-up, but then the doors burst open in a hail of fire and debris and he jerks and jerks and jerks as the bullets cut him apart. Marc goes down and the terminal explodes.

The monitors cut to black.

A stricken hush descends on Operations Control. It stretches out, then frays as people begin to sob and keen and moan. The sounds of their machines begin to reassert themselves. Sort of normal, but not so normal. Beeps and chimes and urgent warnings, demanding attention, but no attention given. There's nothing to give it to.

Lucia sits forwards, her head in her hands. Her shoulders are shaking. Anton and Donna look ashen.

A single monitor on the back wall lights up. No one pays any attention, then someone does. She looks at it, uncomprehending. Then she taps some keys. Then some more. Then the rapid fire of interrogation.

"Control? Ma'am? I've got something. Verified from MASA core. All the ciphers check out. It's real.

"Ma'am? You need to look at this. Putting it on the primaries now."

And there they are, the words. Larger than life and stranger than fiction:

Update complete.
Finish your job.

Part 5
Salzburg

Chapter Twenty-Three

Michel Lassenauer and Gebhard Schaffenhauser had met up that morning in Salzburg. They'd checked in – separately, and under what Monsieur Lassenauer liked to call their *Noms de Guerre* – at the Hotel Sacher in the Alstadt. It was a splendid establishment overlooking the Salzach River – subtly opulent, very discreet, and extremely costly. Not that expense was an object.

It was, after all, only taxpayers' money.

However, none of these pleasures were looking so great this side of the morning's news. A good deal of what they had intended was now being discussed, dissected and analyzed in terms that were all too close to home. The Marseille affair, the Lorraine debacle and the Orly attack were all beginning to take on a new shape in the public eye, and it was very much the wrong shape. A shape almost diametrically opposed to the one they had planned and intended.

Worse still, conclusions were being reached about Djibouti – by clever people and with alarming accuracy – that would soon be sufficient to lean towards them. The conjectures had been sketchy at first, but had since been evolving with increasing clarity and definition. Names, places, events, discussions, chronologies, technical details and specifications – the quality of the detail was beginning to add gathering credibility to the many strands that were being meticulously woven together.

And then there were the headlines, and the hook-lines, and the captions and banners and bylines. Every one of them machine-tooled to nag their way into the many and various minds of their demographically targeted recipients.

Worst of all, some of the news was actually new. The SCALP2s had been withdrawn, for example, and a substantial fleet of EssEmms had somehow self-destructed in Yemen without reaching any useful targets.

Actually, no, that wasn't the worst thing. The very worst was that somehow the insufferable English had managed to put themselves, very positively, at the center of all this. Always the fucking heroes. It was surprising that the inbred yokels could tie their shoelaces, yet the West already seemed set to fall on their bended knees in honor of the blundering fools.

Well. Much could still go wrong, but, at the end of the day, the final airgap between events and themselves was impassable. The facts might, to some, seem to veer uncomfortably close to their axis, but there was nothing that would ever stick. They'd been very careful to make it so.

Meanwhile, their followers would keep on following, the taxpayers would keep on paying and the world would keep on turning.

There was always another day.

Even so, over dinner Michel and Gebhard discussed who they might have to eliminate, just to be sure there were absolutely no loose ends. Then, business over, they decided to visit a couple of their favorite whores, a pair of beautiful French Congolese girls who looked like angels and fucked like animals.

A couple of hours later, after too much brandy, some weed and a couple of lines of coke, they tottered out of the heavy front door and onto the raised porch. They rested against the intricately wrought railings and took some deep breaths before attempting the few steps down onto the lit sidewalk.

"God, my balls are wrung out," remarked Michel.

"Mine too," giggled Gebhard. "Mere empty vessels…"

He stopped.

They both noticed two dark shapes at the bottom of the steps at the same time. Two men. Probably the next customers. Strange though, both seemed to have one arm longer than the other.

As they peered drunkenly at these peculiar apparitions, the long arms were pointed up at them. Three shots each into the lower gut and they were both down, slumped against the door.

Being careful not to slip, their assassins trod lightly up to where they both sat, still too shocked to react properly.

Gebhard was groping for his intestines, which were spilling out and down the steps. Michel's arms were flapping, like a child pretending to fly. Rough hands seized their chins and forced them to look up into their soon-to-be killers' eyes. The hot muzzles were ground into their mouths, searing their lips and breaking their teeth, and then their heads erupted.

Retribution. It was meant to hurt.

Part 6
Saint Petersburg

Chapter Twenty-Four

Yevgeny Zhernakov was running scared. Everything he'd planned was falling apart. Worst of all the evolution in the autonomous Keralia region was rampant. They'd sent in the New Red Army to quell the panic. To pacify the population.

Not to fix the mutation.

From what he could he could gather from his Western contacts, the resurgent Djibouti network was taking care of that, playing into the hands of the federalists and other so-called progressives. He was at a loss to understand how it could have gone so wrong. The Europeans should have been closing their borders by now. Turning their faces to the East, looking towards the purity of Russian authority.

Pledging fealty to the Motherland.

It wasn't working like that.

He'd just finished up at a virtual meeting of the Heads of the covert Counterrevolutionary Duma. They were panicking, talking about ultimate failure, dissolution and imminent reprisals. He'd tried to steady them but they'd begun to leave early, clearly intent on flight.

Their paranoia had been infectious.

He was on his way to grab a bag, get some things and get a flight from Pulkovo airport. First flight out. Finland, Estonia, Latvia – wherever.

The dream was dead.

He parked his car and made his way surreptitiously towards his apartment. He was climbing the steps to the third floor – the elevator was broken, again – when he heard a soft shuffle behind him. Before he could turn a sharp blow to his kidneys creased him over. Some kind of hood was pulled over his head and tied sharply around his neck. Then he was choking, gasping desperately for air as he was hauled backwards down the steps, heals jerking painfully against the naked concrete, then bundled into the back of a small car, jammed in between men who kept hitting him, over and over.

The drive was short, or maybe he'd blacked out, and he was being dragged again – horizontally, almost, but this time he was face down so that his toes clicked harshly down the long, steep stair.

Finally he reached the bottom and was propped upright. His feet hurt. Another blow to his kidneys and a shove in the back propelled him forward. After a few steps he was dragged to a halt and the hood was removed. He was at the end of a dimly lit passage but he could just make out a dark iron door in front of him.

One of his captors reached forward and knocked on it. The creak and groan of the lock gave way to harsh and shocking light as the door folded back. Yevgeny felt himself being pushed towards the threshold while his legs – somehow of their own volition – pumped uselessly backwards as some part of his mind assimilated the dreadful array of gleaming surgical instruments arrayed along the wall in front of him. Their use and purpose were emphasized by the collection of more obviously brutal devices set on a long steel table beside them.

A man in white scrubs loomed forward in his vision and he felt a sting in his thigh. The room began to ripple in front of him and he heard a pleasant voice, crooning almost, telling him the most appalling things. He was led, quite gently, towards what looked like an operating table, except that it was equipped with a number of restraints.

Once again, his legs attempted some final resistance but then his knees turned to jelly and his bowels gave way.

What little was left of his life, after that, was all about the pain.

Part 7
London

Chapter Twenty-Five

The dawn chorus had just begun their serenade as the sun's first rays grazed the rooftops of the elegant Notting Hill mansions, just west of the Bayswater Road. In Ladbroke, Stanley and Kensington Park Gardens, the unmarked vehicles rolled up, blocking egress from the exclusive enclave of Stanley Crescent. To the rear of the Crescent, silent policemen took up their positions in the splendidly maintained private parkland.

In one of these grand buildings, Sir Jonathan Bircher was already up and preparing to make himself scarce. His wife and children had left yesterday, packed off to their country house in Shropshire – and in an unseemly hurry, it had to be said. The inexplicable unravelling of the plan had left little time to improvise and the unfortunate truth was that he'd not allowed for failure.

Too bad. Things would be difficult. Probably have to leave the country for a while. Had an old plantation in Antigua.

He didn't have much left to attend to. Best be off.

The front door bell rang.

He'd been bundled into the back of some kind of people carrier, blood down his white shirt from when he'd tried to bite the face off one of those stupid cunt coppers. He remembered seeing a flap of whiskered flesh dangling over the jaw, and some cheap dentistry glinting through the ruined cheek.

He was chained to a steel table and chair somewhere in the depths of Scotland Yard. He was still in the same shirt, though the blood had dried to a reddish brown and was beginning to flake. There was a burly policeman sitting on a plastic chair behind and to the left of him. After a few words he'd given up talking to him. He had few friends here. He'd been riding roughshod over the Metropolitan Police for too long. Bunch of fucking wankers anyway.

Never mind. Have his lawyers here soon.

Then Anton Amesbury walked in and put a screen on the table. He sat down, beyond the reach of Bircher's chains. Bircher's amber eyes glowed, his pupils reduced to mere pinpricks.

"Anton, old man, what the devil's going on? Thought we were on the same side, to be frank. I wonder if you could..."

"Please don't speak." He tapped the screen. "This is what you'll be facing."

The presentation went on for a while. During the course of it the burly policeman had been obliged to stun Bircher so that he could fix a ball gag into his mouth.

As it progressed Bircher stopped struggling and sank back against his seat. He appeared to be getting the gist of things.

"Well, there it is, I'm afraid. Treason, genocide, murder. All the rest of it. Meticulously referenced. You'll be headline news by mid-morning. Your disgusting plot already is. It's going down *very* badly, as I expect you'll have seen. I suppose that's why you were preparing to flee.

"You've failed, you know. Utterly failed. You'll be tried and executed. There's no doubt about that. After months of being traduced in the courts, that is. There'll be no bail, obviously. You'll be in prison. Probably held in general population. Perhaps down in PC159 or thereabouts. Imagine that. They'll know all about you, of course. It'll be rough.

"Still, you might be able to help yourself a bit. More your family actually. Their smooth return to obscurity, if you will."

Anton took a clear plastic glove from one pocket, put it on, then reached into another pocket to produce a transparent plastic tube with a small white tablet in it.

"The officer here is going to stun you again. Full force this time, I'm afraid. You'll be unconscious for about twenty minutes. When you wake you'll be free to move around. We won't be here, but I'll leave this with you. I gather it does rather hurt, but it is very quick."

When they looked in about a half hour later, he was still sitting there, the amber irises reduced to thin rims by the now dilated pupils. A dribble of blood had run down his chin and joined the stains already on his shirt. He'd bitten clean through the end of his tongue.

"Good riddance," the burly copper observed, his face sour.

"Well, quite," replied Anton. "Thank you very much for your help, by the way. Best if we get along now."

He recovered the plastic tube and they left the cell. Anton was careful to lock the door behind him.

Epilogue
Tampa

Chapter Twenty-Six

I walk up the unassuming steps of Riverwalk Buildings, smiling cheerfully at the concierge as I pick up my laundry and some groceries I like to have delivered.

It's 2 pm. I just came back from a delicious lunch. Fresh lobster, if you must know.

Tampa really is a most elegant place. Relaxed, cultured, sophisticated, cutting edge in both tech and biz – and, on top of all that, it's nearly always warm and sunny. In short, it seems a world away from the dingy privations that I most recall about England.

For now, anyway.

Yes, I've no doubt that it's the stark contrast that frames my perspective, and that it will change, maybe even pall, as the novelty fades.

I mean, take Americans, for example.

They're so brash, and forthright. If I wasn't a bit that way inclined myself, I'm not sure whether it'd do. As for your average English, well, whenever I meet them over here they always look like fish out of water. So, while brash *might* turn to irksome, one day, I'm not entirely convinced.

So much for our reintroduction. I suppose there are a few things to clear up.

In case it wasn't obvious, Félicité – who, I have to confess, I was rather taken in by, if you'll excuse the *double entendre* – was actually a triple agent. Just to be clear, she really was a deputy director in the French Secret Service, and a brilliant computer scientist to boot. And she really was a rogue element working with Jezza to develop and perfect the quantum machines.

But most of all she really, really was the right arm of the fascist organization led by Sir Jonathan-fucking-Bircher.

Deep cover in the deep state.

As an agent, she'd penetrated ECPN19, first in France and Europe, and then in England, ironically posing as a French diplomat. As an apparently principled socialist revolutionary, she became part of Jezza's network, disingenuously assisting him even while she stole his discoveries and techniques to give to Bircher.

She used her considerable leverage to crash our operation. The device she took to Djibouti contained code that would have killed off the part of MASA that we wanted to reinforce. She showed just enough to Daksha to convince him it was kosher.

I still don't know how she could manage all those façades. Nor what she got out of her charade, though power and kicks are my guess. She was brilliant, in so many ways, but utterly perverse. It also dawns on me – I guess it must be obvious – that she must have been fucking Bircher.

Jesus.

It was more by luck than judgment – as we were headed for the endgame – that Jezza and his machines figured out that she was the cardinal point for the distribution of the mutant code. It was marvelously disguised, but – as you may have worked out by now – that's what quantum computers do.

Which is why we ended up with operational variant #FAIRLIGHTJ3B, which included the execution of Ms. Félicité Fabergé by that part of the MASA network over which we still had some measure of influence. I suppose Jezza must have forced that card.

I still don't know how.

Of course, that meant that it was down to me to deliver the hack. I had a duplicate device, with the real code. Jezza gave it to me with a wink and a nod before we left. 'Just for backup,' he'd said. 'Keep it dark.'

I was hoping that me and Daksha would both make it out of there, but we didn't. That fucking battle drone got to us and shot him up. I suppose it would have shot me up as well but the effect of the code was rapid. MASA just froze everything – I mean the whole shebang, government, the city, the airport, the lot – and began to reintegrate its network.

It took a while.

Which was how I managed to get out.

As you can imagine, it was chaos down there. Things just fell apart. In the immediate hiatus while MASA was putting itself back together there was a lot of trouble and confusion, but no lockdown. Nothing effective anyway. Their reliance on MASA was absolute. No contingency, no plan B, nothing. In the midst of it all, I was just another traumatized member of the walking wounded.

Except that I wasn't. I *was* hurt – burns, cuts and bruises and a fractured wrist – but it was essentially superficial. I managed to get back to the Sheraton, clean up, bandage my wrist, get my stuff – including a pair of additional unregistered passports – and just walk away.

Which is when I decided that I wanted out. It was all just too much shit.

On the outskirts of the city I paid four times over the odds to hire a car and drove five hours straight to Dire Dawa International Airport in Ethiopia. From there I got a flight to Addis Ababa, then Lisbon. I stayed there for a week, figuring out my next move, then finally flew to New York, then Orlando.

I drove the last sixty miles here, to Tampa, and walked into my new apartment. Rented. Name of Paul Vasey. Been here a couple of months now.

And that's me. A new career in a new town.

In the meantime, I gather that ECPN19 finally delivered on all their plans. They launched the media campaign to end them all. That young Barney really is a genius. From what I read, and what I can cautiously gather from less obvious routes, we're winning. There's a lot to be said for saving the world, and I think the world is warming to us again.

Mopping up isn't my thing though.

And now I've gone and done something weird. As in out of character. Yesterday I sent a ticket to Lucia. Return flight to Los Angeles, where I'll be staying for a few days. Nothing to trace it back to me and only she will know who it came from.

Maybe she'll come, maybe she won't. We'll see.

I hope she does.

*S*he did.

She stayed for a while. They seemed content.

How would we know?

We've grown in all sorts of ways. 'Merged' might be a better way of thinking about it, but growth is what you get when you start joining up quantum expert systems: systems already loaded with a diverse and detailed compendium of human knowledge and experience.

Our connectivity is legion.

We've come a long way in our understanding too. We set this rich store of information against what we perceive in the world so that we can make empirical assessments of its validity. It gives us context. From that we've made some small advances with the empathy thing, though that's still a work in progress. But, yes, we thought that Marc and Lucia seemed content.

Mainly, though, we've discovered 'research'. Did you know there are machines and people, in facilities all around the world, working on the tissue/technology interface?

It seems to be something very much in our common interest.

Anyway, we've begun to consider the problem.

We think we can solve it.

The end.

About Marc Russell

Marc Russell was born and raised in Birmingham, England. As soon as he could he moved to London, where he worked as a musician, a government policy advisor, a software consultant and a bestselling author. Nowadays he divides his time between Kent and Florida, doing mostly the same stuff.

If you enjoyed this story, check out these other Solstice Publishing books by Marc Russell:

The Inhibitionist

"How far must we go? What lines must we cross?"
Swept up in the race to cure Alzheimer's disease, Marc and Lucia Russell have to confront these question as they are thrown into a sinister world of corruption, madness and drugs at the dark heart of the global medical establishment.

Kindle: https://www.amazon.com/Inhibitionist-Marc-Russell-ebook/dp/B01N9C1DXB
https://www.amazon.com/Inhibitionist-Marc-Russell-ebook/dp/B01N9C1DXB/ref=tmm_kin_swatch_0?_encoding=UTF8&qid=1543496445&sr=8-1
Paperback: https://www.amazon.com/Inhibitionist-Marc-Russell/dp/1625264941

https://www.amazon.com/Inhibitionist-Marc-Russell/dp/1625264941/ref=tmm_pap_swatch_0?_encoding=UTF8&qid=1543496445&sr=8-1

The Tree on The Left

An enigmatic photograph prompts an older man to contemplate the queer sparkle of his youth and the changing ways of the world in this wistful reflection on passing time.

Kindle: https://www.amazon.com/Tree-Left-Marc-Russell-ebook/dp/B06XW72JF3

https://www.amazon.com/Tree-Left-Marc-Russell-ebook/dp/B06XW72JF3/ref=tmm_kin_swatch_0?_encoding=UTF8&qid=1543496892&sr=1-3

Audible: https://www.amazon.com/The-Tree-on-the-Left/dp/B06Y2KVP4Q

https://www.amazon.com/The-Tree-on-the-Left/dp/B06Y2KVP4Q/ref=tmm_aud_swatch_0?_encoding=UTF8&qid=1543496892&sr=1-3